# Black Book on the
# *Welsh Theatre*

### *(The Early Years 1947-1995)*

## *Volumes I, II, III, IV, V collected*

### *by*

# *Dedwydd Jones*

For Brian Cox
Hwyl,
Dedwydd

Paperback ISBN 978-1-909049-11-6

*Foreword by* **JAN MORRIS**

## Acknowledgements

For articles and, letters, I am indebted to:

The Stage and Television Today

The Times

The Western Mail

Punch

Thanks also due to:

The National Library of Wales

The Mander and Mitchenson Picture Collection

The BBC Hulton Picture Gallery

The Western Mail and Echo

For computers, thank you to:

Saurabh Sethi
Maruti M. Morajkar
Sujatha Sahay

Front and back cover:

Celtic warrior two-headed tombstone, one facing life, the other, death.

Roquepertuse, Bouches-du-Rhone, France

# Foreword

Nobody has fought harder for a dignified, lively and honourable theatre in Wales than Dedwydd Jones, the author of this angry book. As playwright, as polemicist, as irrepressible arguer, he has himself been a living exemplar of what a theatrical tradition ought to be. His opponents have been varied and many, but in particular he has always tilted his lance against the bureaucratic pillars of what passes as the theatrical Establishment in Wales. I share his strong feelings. It seems to me that there are only two legitimate purposes for Welsh national theatre. The first is to encourage the vitality of the indigenous culture, by performing Welsh plays of the past, and by giving a stage to Welsh playwrights and actors of the present. The second is to present to Welsh people plays of the highest possible international standards -- plays from the international repertoire. As I understand it, these are Dedwydd's convictions too, and his noble battle for them, against heavy odds and much discouragement, is an object lesson to us all.

**Jan Morris**

# Contents:

## VOLUME 1:

**Letters to the Press:1974 - 1983**

(In chronological order)


**Outline Plan for Welsh Drama**

1975 to the present day


*End of Volume 1*


**Black Book Volume II, lost to the world**

**Black Book Volume III, 1985-1987, *'Dollops'***

**Black Book Volume IV, 1988-1990 *'Asides.'***

**Black Book Volume V, 1991-1995 *'The Charmer of Splott'***

# George Bernard Shaw,
# on a Welsh National Theatre

G. B. Shaw "Wales must have the best drama that Wales can produce"

## Theatre's Role and Function:

**" Wales must have the best drama that Wales can produce"**

There are two things that may as well be said at the outset somewhat firmly about the proposed Welsh national theatre. If it succeeds it will not be a place for ebullition of patriotic sentiment and flattery of local self-sufficiency. On the contrary, it will be rather a place of humiliation and penitence, relieved by laughter and tears. The Irish have a national theatre, and a conspicuously successful one. But its earlier performances had often to be protected by the police. Mr Yeats's *Countess Kathleen* roused all the latent bigotry of Dublin against it. Synge's *Playboy of the Western World* produced a fortnight's rioting, and, though an admitted masterpiece of the national literature, still provokes explosions of wounded Irish conceit. The peasant hero of one of Mr Lennox Robinson's plays makes his most effective exit with the words, "I hate Ireland."

Everything that is narrow and ignorant and ridiculous and dishonest in Wales will be castigated ruthlessly by the Welsh national theatre, and the process will not be popular with the narrow, the ignorant, the bigoted and the ridiculous. Over the border nobody cares enough about Wales (why should they?) to tell her the truth about herself --to rub into her conscience the glaring faults of her striking qualities. If Wales thinks that a national theatre will be a place where her praises are sounded continually, where the male villain will be an

Englishman of the Church of England, and the female villain a French spy or a bishop's wife, whilst the hero (being a Welshman) will be insufferably noble, and the heroine (being a Welshwoman) too good for this earth, Wales will be disappointed. Just as the preachers of Wales spend much of their time in telling the Welsh that they are going to hell, so the Welsh writers of comedy will have to console a good many of them by demonstrating that they are not worth wasting good coal on. If it be really true that Wales is in so benighted a condition that ministers are still to be found there who not only do not go to the theatre, but try to prevent other people from going, forgetting that a theatre is a place where two or three are gathered together, and that God fulfils himself in many ways without consulting the local clergy, I venture **to remind these walkers in darkness** that if they strangle Welsh theatre in its cradle, they will have, not a country without a theatre, but a country delivered over wholly to the crude cinematograph melodramas of the American and Italian film makers, and to musical comedies on tour from London. In Scotland in the seventeenth century, and in Geneva under Calvin, all theatrical enterprise was stopped; and the result was what Knox called "a school of Christ", meaning, in fact, a place where joyless people hated their joyless neighbours, and cared for nothing except making money, refusing to speak to or associate with people with twenty pounds a year or less than themselves.

Such a state of things is no longer possible. If Wales will not have the best that Wales can produce she will get the worst that the capitals of Europe can produce;

a long-standing enemy, a local lawyer, had seized Twm's mother's home in lieu of her son's past debts and had turned her out into the cold. In rage, Twm wrote to the lawyer "in brimstone and fire." The letter so unnerved his enemy, the house was returned and the debt overlooked.

Twm then built his own house and re-established himself in business, this time as a brick-layer, oven-engineer, and "smoke doctor." But his pen was as busy as ever. For the first (and last) time, he decided to compete for the bardic crown, the summit of a Welsh writer's achievement. He entered work in the 1789 Corwyn "Eisteddfod" Wales's National Festival of Poetry. The adjudicators, however, thoroughly disapproved of their lowly, native-born, gadfly-playwright. Twm was still very much the rebel-peasant-subversive, with an extremely unpleasant tongue. Moreover, he possessed none of the formal qualifications needed for entry into the "best" Welsh social circles. The crown was awarded to a "safe" academic, Walter Mechain of Jesus College, Oxford. However, one of the adjudicators, Dr. Samwell (formerly Captain Cook's ship's doctor) personally presented a silver quill to "the Cambrian Shakespeare," as he called Twm. This was exaggerated praise certainly, but Twm treasured the gift and Dr Samwell's kindness for the rest of his life.

Twm remained vigorous into old age and "was never once ill in my life, except when a loaded cart ran over my belly." He selected his own tombstone and carved his name and epitaph on it. He worked to the day of his death, for, as he said, "There's no work in the grave." He was buried in Denbigh and was deeply mourned by the people he had championed, loved and inspired. His work, however, was confined to oblivion by the establishment he had so fearlessly criticized. Even today you can meet Welshmen casually in the pubs of Denbigh who will tell you stories of the great People's Champion and his "Interludes" as if he had lived but yesterday.

Punch,

March 3rd, 1974

# A Welshman man who was No Saint"

## A Swiss View

The English have Shakespeare; the Welsh - Thomas Edwards, known as Twm O'r Nant. Twm O'r Nant was a peasant-poet dramatist who fought against the importation of English cultural fashions into his country. It was the kind of struggle against imperialist domination which became widespread in many small countries at the end of the eighteenth century. In Dedwydd Jones's play *Bard,* the character of Twm O'r Nant and the times he lived in, are powerfully and vividly evoked.

There was nothing in Twm O'r Nant's background to suggest his extraordinary destiny. He was of peasant stock. In his whole life, he received only two weeks of formal schooling. Yet by the age of nine, he had already completed hundreds of poems. Lacking the means to buy real ink, he used the juice of elderberries. The wild elderberry fits in well with the image of a native poet of the soil striving to give life to his own theatre, a theatre almost submerged by the mass of frivolous, light-weight dramas brought in from London. Twm's strictures obviously offended the notables who chose to impose such plays but Twm was profoundly respected by his fellow-countrymen, especially by the small-holders and peasants whose labours were being exploited by outsiders solely for profit. Twm O'r Nant lived through a period when England was establishing a vast overseas colonial Empire as well as subduing non-English populations closer to home. Hence Twm O'r Nant wrote of matters affecting all colonies of the day --tolls, duties, taxes and social and political repression.

Harvey Granville-Baker, 1900, English champion of Welsh Drama

## In Celtic Lands

To re-create the second half of the eighteenth century and the great Welsh folk-hero it produced, Dedwydd Jones has written an intensely visual scenario, but one which, happily, is ideally adaptable to radio. He uses flash-backs, documentary effects and fantasy to bring the protagonist to life. Dedwydd Jones, in keeping with the folk-theatre Twm was attempting to foster, introduces authentic local characters (the Squire and the Parson, for example), as well as more mythical, traditional Welsh figures such as the Lord Death. We find ourselves indeed in a Celtic community, a community that always refers to its archaic past and ancient lore in its struggle for survival. *Bard* is one of some thirty plays that Dedwydd Jones has written in the past twenty years. Although he is now domiciled in Switzerland --he lectures at Lausanne's College of Commerce –he is still working to establish and promote a Welsh National Theatre in his homeland. It might be said that he has been somewhat more successful in this than his own great hero, Twm O'r Nant, for Dedwydd Jones has had plays produced not only in Wales and England, but also in the USA and on the Continent. Roland Jay produced the play for Swiss radio. His adaptation catches all the rough vigour and colour of the original. The masterly translation is by Algerian-born Danielle Obadia, who now also lives in Lausanne.

Translated from the Swiss Radio and TV Times

23rd Sept., 1982.

# The Founders of Welsh Theatre

## *(1911-1952)*

If Twm O'r Nant was the father of Welsh drama, the founders of modern Welsh theatre are the writers Caradoc Evans and Richard Hughes, the playwright JO Francis, and, in radio drama, the poet Dylan Thomas.

There are four plays which typify Welsh dramatic writing: *Change* (1911) by JO Francis; *A Comedy of Good and Evil* (1924) by Richard Hughes; *Taffy* (1923) by Caradoc Evans, and *Under Milkwood* (1952) by Dylan Thomas.

All four plays share certain characteristics which are distinctively Welsh. These are a reverence for the great mysteries of existence (God, love, death, nature), a love of words, a love of strong emotion, egalitarianism, a sympathy for women, and an intense attachment to Welsh roots.

The most signifigant feature of the plays is that they reflect nothing of the English Class System, either in the society they depict or in the accents they employ. This must be plainly stated because of the limitations of the English Theatre in Wales and its often damaging influence on the course of Welsh drama.

Without the identification of accent, English audiences soon become restive --"Just what class of person *are* they?" The characters in *Under Milkwood,* for example, are unidentifiable in English class terms. They are, therefore, all too readily accepted as caricatures and become quaint, folksy, Welsh stereotypes. That there **is** only one accent in Wales is often overlooked. The accent, for example, of Polly Garter in *Under Milkwood* (1952), and the collier Price in *Change* (1911), are identical. The characters in these plays are "well-spoken" only if they are articulate and "educated" only if their language is informed. The accent-distinctions of "upper-class" Royal Shakespeare Company Oxbridge, are absent; nor is there any place for the "lower-class" accents of Stratford East, or the "middle-class" suburbanite tones of Ayckbourn. Thus, in Welsh drama, accent does not determine social position or character. Each character exists, first and foremost, in human terms. The Welsh accent is egalitarian. (In an obituary on the late Richard Burton it was pointed out that Burton felt considerable unease during his days at Stratford. Burton's strictures on audiences there are well known. This unease has been cited as one reason for his non-return to the "English" theatre.)

The second limitation of the English Theatre in Wales, is that it does not adapt to the Celt and his love of deep and rapid changes of emotion. This deficiency is analysed with great insight by Norman Marshall in his remarkable *The Other Theatre* a history of fringe (or "progressive") theatre in the thirties. Marshall examines, in particular, the work of the Irish Director JB Fagan at the Oxford Playhouse. Fagan first introduced Chekov to Oxford audiences, and other Slav and Celtic dramatists. Marshall comments: "The Slav and the Celt share a natural melancholy, a quality which the Englishman finds difficult to understand. He usually confuses it with mere gloominess and depression. English producers of Chekov, misunderstanding the true quality of melancholy, and fearing that the play may seem gloomy to the audience, usually overstress the humour at the expense of the other and deeper emotions." And: "The intrusion of farce at the most unexpected moments is apt to bewilder English audiences. They lack the mental and emotional agility to move swiftly from one emotion to another without warning. This agility - call it emotional instability if you prefer - is a quality as Celtic as it is Slav." JO Francis, whose plays were produced by Fagan at Oxford, was well aware of this disability. Sam, the cockney in Francis's play *Change,* warns the Price family: "There's a lot too much feelings about for comfort. If yer wants to be happy in this world, yer got to keep yer feelings down. "The Welsh Theatre, then, if it is to find an independent place in European drama, must trust to its own emotional resources and establish theatres which are directed predominantly by Celts. The love of the great mysteries, especially of "God" (in the widest possible sense) in man and in nature, passionately suffuses all four plays. It is no surprise, therefore, that the loveliest and most moving poem in *Under Milkwood* is given to a clergyman, the Rev. Eli Jenkins. In *Taffy,* too, the culminating speech is delivered by a rebel preacher. The protagonist of *A Comedy of Good and Evil* is a Rector. *Change* is as concerned about old Chapel values as it is about miners' pay. Good and evil, too, is conceived in farcical terms, as in Richard *Hughes's Comedy of Good and Evil.* The dialogue here is mainly between Lucifer and Gabriel. Lucifer is represented by the eldrich Gladys (who is given the only English accent in the play!) and Owain Flatfish, "the plain-clothes guardian-angel of the district." These two forces struggle for the possession of the Rector's soul. The women's roles –the diabolic

Gladys and Minnie, the Rector's wife-- are as important as the men's. There is an easy balance between male and female. In *Taffy*, the struggle is between the spirit that went into the making of the first chapel, "... built on a moor... by love... where no one lost his way or went in vain," and the degenerate, contemporary "Big Heads" (deacons), who "burrow like swine in Sion", who "stink of evil" and whose pulpit is the "trap-door to helL" Again it is a woman, Marged, who is the real heroine. It is her fearlessness and determination which convinces her man to quit the "unholy" orders.

Edith Evans memorably created the part in the first production in 1923.

The conflict in JO Francis's *Change* is between the economic forces of good and evil. The play is a mirror of old radical Wales. One of collier Price's sons rails: "Look at the place we're living in mean streets, mean homes, mean chapels, mean pubs. On and on the people go... breeding children who will grow up in the same old senseless round --unless we change it now. Change it!" The story centres on the great miners' strike of 1911. But the longed-for "change" never comes. The Empire of Evil (Industrial-Capitalism) wins in the end.

In the tragedy of the family, the collier's wife, Gwen, is given equal prominence. Gwen sees her sons violently killed, dead of disease, or dispersed. The hopelessness of the colliers' womenfolk is as fairly represented as the despair of the striking miners.

However, *Under Milkwood* joyfully eludes all such conflicts, for all the "No Good Boyos" have opted out --"I don't know who's up there and I don't care." The play is a lyrical celebration of Welsh life. The Rev. Eli Jenkins is Chief Bard and his songs of praise embrace all Wales.

Edith Evans in the first production of *Taffy*, 1923

By Cader Idris,tempest-torn,

Or Moel yr Wyddfa's glory,

Carnedd Llewelyn beauty born,

Plinlimmon old in story,


By mountains where King Arthur dreams,

By Penmaenmawr defiant,

Llaregyb Hill a molehill seems,

A pygmy to a giant.


By Carreg Cennen, King of Time,

Our Heron Head is only

A bit of stone with seaweed spread

Where gulls come to be lonely.

In *Milkwood,* it is nature and human nature which finally triumph.

Of the four plays, it is *Milkwood* which best illustrates the Welsh love of the music of words. From the opening lines,"....it is Spring, moonless night... starless and bible-black... ", the poet at once sets on display the riches within. But eloquent speeches are found in all the plays, as in Richard Hughes's *Comedy:* "Death! There are some who imagine death as a person, a rider, an ancient man at the heads of armies... but I saw death as a butterfly of dark-coloured glass who sips at our hearts. Mother Death --the dark blossom of Golgotha!"

*A Comedy of Good and Evil* was first produced in Wales on BBC radio in 1952. It was promptly denounced as "blasphemous, anti-Christ and satanic!" - strange recognition for the man who had written the world's first ever "listening play", *Danger,* commissioned by the fledgling BBC in January, 1924.. The names of the characters in the plays are also peculiarly vivid, "Scraggy Evans the Post, Owain Flatfish - Guardian Angel, Mrs Resurrection Jones, Attila Rees, Powell the Stockings, Lord Cut-Glass, Josi Stonemason, Essec Coffin-Maker, Captain Shacob, Captain Cat." There are numerous Reverends, from the famous Eli Jenkins to the more obscure Reverend "Tearful" Watkins, whose sermons are "Soul-ticklers." These nick-names are not only striking in themselves, they also reveal a special regard for the distinguishing qualities of individual identity. When the plays were first produced, they were at once recognized as contributing something original and exciting to drama in general. Caradoc Evans was called "The English(!) Gorki". Frank Swinnerton commented, "The most striking thing in English (!) letters." The Weekly Dispatch (London), "The characters have the weaknesses of humanity rather than of class or sect." The Westminster Gazette,"... unmatched since Swift." The Sketch (London) was somewhat bewildered, "It is a picture of life in parts of this little island which are definitely farther away than Paris or New York." Of *Change,* Town Topics (New York), "A drama which fell into line with the best of modern writing." The Mail (Montreal), "An excellent addition to dramatic literature." Of *A Comedy of Good and Evil* GB Shaw wrote, "Anyone who cannot enjoy all this must be an idiot!" One year after its first performance, *Under Milkwood* was established as a classic. It remains Wales's most loved and most performed play.

The four founding fathers of Welsh theatre therefore did full justice to Wales and to their own natural Celtic feeling and character. It is now up to the new generation of playwrights, in their turn, to collect, uncompromisingly, the rich, ungathered harvests of Welsh history and life which lie in such abundance about them. It is vital, too, to find directors whose background and outlook would provide the right insight into the heart of such new "native" plays. The last word must go to a great Englishman of the theatre, Harley Granville-Barker, who stated during a debate in support of a project for a Welsh National Theatre, "The greatest service Wales can render the world is to be herself to the last drop of her blood."

Dylan Thomas reading, 1950

# Welsh National Drama

## The Early Days

Wales continues its unique search for a genuine national drama, a search that has become somewhat exotic of late. Its method now is first to ignore the Welsh drama that already exists and, thereafter, to keep on constructing Million-Pound-Theatre Complexes as unassailable proofs of this nonexistence. As a result of this rare logic, Wales is now studded with Million-Pound-Theatre-Complexes which stand as testaments to absolutely nothing. Do empty graves really require such lavish Cenotaphs? The answer must, apparently, be yes. But is the old grave that this new monument is supposed to honour, really empty? Has anyone bothered to check the alleged corpse of Welsh Drama? Well, G.B.Shaw, for one, thought it worth a look.

"Bernard Shaw on Welsh Drama. Brilliant and Witty Article; Theatre's Role and Function" --headlines in the South Wales Daily Post, Saturday, June 13, 1914.

Shaw's "brilliant and witty" article was written in support of "Lord Howard de Walden's Company of Welsh Players, in plays by Welshmen, at the Swansea Grand Theatre, during the week commencing the 29th inst... "

Shaw was optimistic: "If Manchester, Dublin and Glasgow produced, as they did, an indigenous drama almost instantly 19 upon... the establishment of a theatre... What Might Wales Not Do, with its wealth of artistic faculty... its great gift of imagination and adventurousness... and its sense of nationality?"

31

The answer to that is --nothing. For all that is "indigenous" about them, the "Welsh" theatres of today might as well advertise their wares in the Neasden Evening News. The (now defunct) so-called "Welsh" Theatre Company alone, for example, spent over one and a half million pounds since its inception in 1962. It produced not one original indigenous play, not one original indigenous dramatist, and not one original indigenous programme of plays, of any real merit, in the entire thirteen years of its existence.

And the consequences of de Walden's failure? "If... those walkers in darkness strangle the Welsh National Theatre in its cradle, they will have not a country without a theatre but a country delivered over wholly to the crude melodramas... of the film-makers and to musical comedies on tour from London... if he (a Welshman)... finds a national theatre there (in Wales), he will become a poet. If not, he will have to drift to London, as I had to drift from Dublin to London (there was no Irish National Theatre in my day), and produce the stuff London likes, as best he can." Shaw's "drift to London" is now a stampede and the "musical comedies on tour from London" are an epidemic in Wales.


## Humiliation and Penitence

Shaw continues: "If the Theatre succeeds, it will not be... a place of flattery of local self-sufficiency... or a place where Wales's praises will be sounded continuously... on the contrary, it will be rather a place of humiliation and penitence, relieved by laughter and tears... everything that is narrow and ignorant and ridiculous and dishonest in Wales will be castigated ruthlessly by the Welsh National Theatre, and the process will not be popular with the narrow, the ignorant, the bigoted and the ridiculous." But was Wales "in so benighted a condition" that she became Shaw's dustbin of drama? Yes, she did. And still is. With one exception - Caradoc Evans - "the great Caradoc Evans" as Dylan Thomas called him.

One of the main battles of Caradoc's own Great Welsh Uprising took place in, irony of ironies, the Prince of Wales Theatre, London, on February 26th, 1923, with the help of his play *Taffy*. How the faithful London Welsh packed the theatre at the first performance, and how their faithful jeers, catcalls and howls nearly brought the performance to a riotous halt. Police were finally called in and the play drew to a close amidst continued "explosions of wounded (Welsh) conceit." Wales's great Castigator had again been "telling Wales the truth about herself" and this time in a public place, in a theatre, and in London! What would the English neighbours say?

Caradoc's first book, *My People* (1915), had been described in the Welsh Press as "foul garbage", "literature of the sewer", and·Caradoc himself as having "a mind like a sexual pigsty." Wales's national newspaper stated, "The final feeling on finishing this book is to have a good bath." The Chief Constable of Cardiff chimed in with a sublime comment, "I was 20 years at Scotland Yard and I read most of the suppressed books and *My People* is the worst book I have ever read." And Lloyd George, especially Lloyd George, decided: "Pride of race now belongs to the lowest savage. This man is a renegade!" But what did the English say? Hugh Walpole, "The most striking thing in English (!) Letters." Frank Swinnerton, "An artist who is as ruthless as Balzac." Thomas Burke, "The English (!) Gorki."

At home, however, Caradoc was soon feted as "the most hated man in Wales." And what of the fate of *Taffy* itself? The Pall Mall Magazine, "There is more good stuff in *Taffy* than we will find in half a dozen of our varnished, service-flat plays." The English Review, "We left more alive than when we entered the Theatre." The Westminster Gazette, "The reputation of Mr Evans as a satirist of his own people unmatched in English Literature since Swift, drew intellectual and artistic London in ranks to hear *Taffy.*" The Daily Telegraph, "The most merciless and outspoken critic of Welsh life and character that has yet arisen." The Observer, The Times, The Nation and The Sunday Express were all equally lavish in their praise. The Spectator came closest to the truth, "It is easy to accuse Mr Evans of being rude to his mother (Wales) but his vilification of the Southern Welsh is the outcome of his love for Wales." What? This "foul garbage" an "outcome of love"? Blasphemy now! The Spectator continued, "Further performances of *Taffy* should have a considerable success." Further performances?! Of a "savage and a renegade in a sexual pigsty"? Never in Wales!

Richard Hughes, a founder of Welsh Drama

## Vilification of Evans

Wales instead intensified its vilification of Caradoc. His books were banned from Welsh libraries. He had to have police protection when he gave public lectures, even in Cambridge! Of his great novel, *Nothing to Pay* (1930), a Welsh review stated: "This is a dirty book. We prefer to call it filth." Caradoc was even accused of creating the bad image which the English had of the Welsh. After Caradoc's death in 1945, the abuse still continued. A Welsh obituary notice stated, "He set an example to a rising school of Welsh writers in English to bend and peer under stones."

A member of this "rising school" was Dylan Thomas, whose favourite play was, yes, *Taffy.* (One wonders if Dylan ever read Caradoc's *The Humour and Pathos of Welsh Vii/age Life,* published in 1907). And after the obituaries, Caradoc was given a second and extremely prolonged interment by special arrangement with Wales's very own "Walkers in Darkness." Since Caradoc's death, only *My People* has been re-printed in Wales.

All Caradoc's other works, including *Taffy,* are unobtainable. As for *Taffy,* to this day (1976), the play has never been performed at any theatre, at any time whatsoever, anywhere in Wales.

And what was Caradoc's response to all these obscenities? "I tell violent truths," he stated. "Wales knows that it is true." And --a comment of some finality-- "I told the truth and it was the stinking truth." Caradoc saw his work as "clearing the money-lenders from the temple." The money-lenders were the deacons, the elders, the teachers and wealthy members of the Chapel, who, in unholy alliance, "keep the people down and chase away the living God," --like "Nanni", a typical victim, who died on a diet of rats, her last halfpenny squeezed out of her by a greedy and tyrannical preacher. "Flattery of local self-sufficiency?" Never for Caradoc. Having told "the stinking truth" about *My People,* Caradoc went on to *My Neighbours,* his London "neighbours" this time, the London Welsh. Here Caradoc found the same bigotry to revile, the same greed, ignorance, intolerance and hypocrisy, and the same tyrannical Chapel. He castigates them all, including - the ultimate insult - his neighbours' newest God, Lloyd George, the Great Boyo himself, "that rampant and hypocrital satyr!" "A savage and a renegade!" thundered back Lloyd George ("Ben Lloyd" in the book!), while the English Asquiths, having "much enjoyed *Taffy",* invited Caradoc to tea!

### Indigenous Drama

How "the stinking truth" got through! And the humiliation of it! Wales's cosy, folksy image had been blown, and it had been blown "in the other language", too, in English, and in such perfect English that even the respectable English reviewers had been taken in by "the savage" in his "sexual pigsty." How Caradoc "rubbed into the Welsh conscience, the glaring defects of her finer qualities." How Caradoc really "cared" and how he recognised that "no one over the border really did care about Wales." And how Wales never forgave him. The humiliation, the penitence, the castigation, all the Shavian elements were there. Wales, for the first time in

English, was offered its own indigenous drama. Wales "got the best that Wales could produce" and Wales promptly buried the lot.

*Taffy,* in fact, represents Wales's own forgotten native drama. One wonders, therefore, just how many more Million-Pound-Theatre Complexes must be thrown up in Wales in order to house again just one honest, real, truthful *Taffy,* and to recognise, once and for all, that the first genuine national Welsh Drama was born near Shaftesbury *Avenue* on February 26th, 1923, and that the true corpse is not Welsh Drama, but the vain and hollow monuments of Wales's own "Walkers in Darkness."

The Stage, March 1976

# The Lost Renaissance

## The Welsh Theatre Must Learn to unbury its dead

Caradoc Evans contemplating "My People"

On January 15th, 1924, the world's first "listening play", *Danger* went on the air. It was commissioned by the BBC, written by Richard Hughes and produced by Nigel Playfair. Almost exactly one year earlier, on February 26th, 1923 Caradoc Evans's play *Taffy,* produced by Miles Maleson, had established the fact of a new indigenous Welsh drama. The twenties were indeed the cradle of a Welsh renaissance. In the same year, 1924, Richard Hughes wrote *A Comedy* of *Good and Evil,* which was first produced at the Court Theatre by the remarkable Mrs. Whitworth on July 6th, 1924. One critic, GB Shaw, an old champion of Welsh drama -indeed, of any "genuine indigenous drama"-- wrote an article on Hughes's play which concluded, "Anyone who cannot enjoy all this must be an idiot." When the play was performed at the Lyric, Hammersmith, under Nigel Playfair's direction, it provided comparisons with Synge and the Abbey Theatre.

Next, JB Fagan, the most astonishing of all the "fringe" producers of the twenties, selected *A Comedy of Good and Evil,* produced it at The Playhouse, Oxford and then brought it in March, 1925 to the Ambassador's Theatre, London. Norman Marshall, in his excellent history of the theatre between the wars, *The Other Theatre,* lists Hughes's play, with the first ever production of *The Cherry Orchard* in England, as "the most vivid of JB Fagan's productions of that season." At the same time, another Welshman, again of somewhat unusual talent, was having his first play produced. The play was *The Rat* and the author, the glamorous David Ivor Davies, better known as Ivor Novello. JB Fagan then produced a first play by a young Welsh undergraduate at Oxford. The play, *Full Moon* and the author, Emlyn Williams.

The Stage, March 1976

Donald Houston in *Under Milkwood, 1956*

Fagan went even further. He rescued one of Wales's earliest abandoned talents, JO Francis. In 1910, Francis had written *Change,* a remarkable chronicle, by any standards, of industrial strife in South Wales. The play was eventually performed by the Incorporated Stage Society at the Haymarket Theatre in December, 1913. It was then taken up, or rather, taken back to Wales by the English Lord Howard de Walden, director of Wales's first short-lived Welsh National Drama Company. *Change* was performed at the Cardiff New Theatre in May,1914. It was this production which inspired

Granville-Barker and GB Shaw to pledge their support for a "genuine indigenous Welsh National Drama." De Walden then toured *Change* in the USA. Ainslee's Magazine (New York) said of it, "The best play written... and produced for many seasons." The Clarion (New York), "A truly wonderful piece of work." The Mail (Montreal), "An excellent addition to dramatic literature."

Who could now gainsay the renaissance? Wales did. De Walden's Company soon disbanded. *Change* was consigned to its Celtic burial-chamber and there it has rested for over sixtyfive years. But Fagan produced Francis's next play *The Beaten Track* during his last season at the Oxford Playhouse. After that, the curtain finally did come down. The little renaissance had been born in Oxford and London, but Wales had somehow mislaid it. The twenties were, therefore, both the cradle and the grave of Welsh drama. Thereafter, the dramatists, sufficiently discouraged by their own valley funerals, turned away from the theatre to concentrate on prose.

The thirties now saw the glitter and triumph of Ivor Novello and Emlyn Williams. However, faint flickers of the hard old Shavian drama were still seen. In 1937, Norman Marshall revived *A Comedy of Good and Evil* at the famous Gate Theatre of which he had become director. Caradoc Evans, in desperate straits for money, revived *Taffy* in 1939. "Wife puts on play to save writer from prison," proclaimed the headlines.

However, the strangest reappearance, and possibly the last, of *A Comedy of Good and Evil,* was in Scotland under the banner of a "decentralized" national Scottish drama, led by James Bridie. James Bridie had founded The Citizens' Theatre in 1943. He believed that Scotland was a "good laboratory for decentralized experiments," because "Scotland has never been thoroughly centralized, either in spirit or in fact and it has never had a theatre of its own." Bridie, too, encouraged indigenous drama, "We have always associated showmanship with London... and to the London idiom in playwriting." In his season of plays, therefore, Bridie placed *A Comedy of Good and Evil* among "the plays of other nations" (between Gogol and Massinger, in fact), a late but lasting tribute to the little renaissance (however overlooked in Wales) and to the labours of Shaw, Fagan, Barker and to all the other great names of the English theatre, who had helped foster it. Ironically, even after the Welsh obsequies on its own writers had faded, Dylan Thomas, at the end of his own brief "renaissance", unexpectedly created what is possibly the greatest of "listening plays", *Under Milkwood,* first seen, of course, outside Wales.

In this year of the devolution referendum, one wonders about the fate of new "genuine indigenous" drama and dramatists, anywhere. Certainly for Wales, one thing is definite --there is no real future for Welsh drama until the Welsh theatre unburies its dead and the plays of Caradoc Evans, Richard Hughes and JO Francis are seen to be what they truly are-- the living foundation for a genuine Welsh National Drama.

The Stage, March 1977.

# Welsh National Theatre Projects

## 1950-60

From the first decade of the century to the outbreak of the Second World War, numerous brave attempts were made to establish a Welsh National Theatre. After the war, the idea slowly revived. The fifties ushered in a period particularly rich in Welsh theatre talent and with the support of such star names as Richard Burton and Stanley Baker, the national theatre movement was launched once again.

Promises of help poured in. Encouragement even came from the Arts Council of Great Britain which officially sanctioned the new initiative. Donations were slower to arrive but by 1959, the leading organisers had raised the initial capital and the St David's Trust was founded. Its principal officers were actors Clifford Evans and Meredith Edwards. Meredith Edwards provided the link with Lord Howard De Walden's pre-war Welsh national theatre projects. The Trust at once announced its main aim --the founding of a Welsh National Theatre.

At the same time, Welsh drama was enjoying a mini renaissance in London with the plays of Gwyn Thomas, Dannie Abse, Alun Owen and Alun Richards.

In Wales in 1962, the Welsh Committee of the Arts Council of Great Britain (WCAC), launched its first theatre company in Cardiff, the Welsh Drama Company (WDC) but it had no theatre of its own.

Richard Burton helped early theatre ventures in Wales

The aims of these three bodies, the St David's Trust, the Welsh Drama Company and the Welsh Committee of the Arts Council, seemed identical. However, by the mid-seventies, the grand design for a Welsh National Theatre was a ghastly and ignominious ruin. How and why? The blame lies squarely with the three protagonists, or, antagonists, as they soon became.

Firstly, the St David's Trust. This had been set up outside Wales. It appeared to be dominated by rich and autocratic exiles. Official bodies and theatre enthusiasts in Wales were fearful of being overruled by a powerful non-resident minority. Unfortunately, the Trust's first announcements did little to allay these fears. The Trust saw the new national theatre as a counterpart to London's projected National Theatre on the South Bank --whose existence was still only marked by a solitary foundation stone. Wales's new national theatre was to be just as huge and complex. The theatre shell itself was modelled on the multi-purpose Civic Theatre at Frankfurt-am-Main, which, in 1960, boasted a staff of over three hundred. Overweening Welsh vanity was soon wedded to this irrelevant gigantism. Gilded roll-calls of Wales's crowned bards were planned for the luxurious foyer. Fund-raising was to be inaugurated at a Grand Wales-Patagonia Ball at the London Hilton in the presence of the Argentinian Ambassador. This modest little soiree, however, failed to materialize. A second Grand Ball was later proposed, this time with Prince Charles, fresh from his Caernarvon Investiture hit, in the lead. Thankfully, neither spectacle got beyond the invitation-list stage. Such grisly functions are typical of the dirge-like Welsh yearning for respectability. Any future Welsh theatre plans are certain to be cursed by similar empty solemnities and national conceits. The fatal weakness of the Trust's plans lay not only in its vanities and impracticalities, but also in its failure to identify with any recognizable Welsh community, Welsh or English-speaking. The Trust had already created ineradicable suspicions by opting for the grandiose, the imitative and the prestigious. Its increasingly remote deliberations now took place in the rarefied retreats of chairmen and committees, aldermen and academics. The wishes of the public, which, after all, forms the bulk of any audience, were neither considered nor consulted. The dramatists, whose work would *have* provided the link between a Welsh theatre and its community, were also ignored. But despite this palpable falling short of objectives, the Trust continued to lavish thousands on plans which *never* got off the drawing board. These *even* included a domed national theatre on wheels.

Meanwhile, the new Welsh Drama Company, already famed for its numbing auditorium-emptying tours of Wales, persisted – like a blight. By its weird choice of plays, it, too, had alienated popular support. It, too, had failed to tie in with the community. It, too, ignored its own dramatists and actors who remained marooned in London. But the Welsh Theatre Company blamed its failure on the lack of a permanent base. It had no theatre. It therefore cast envious eyes on the majestic edifices proposed by the St David's Trust. The Welsh Drama Company, was, it seemed, ready-made to occupy Wales's first national theatre.

The Welsh Committee of the Arts Council appeared to concur. The Trust, however,, vehemently repudiated all such take-over bids - although, as yet, there was nothing to take over. The Welsh Committee of the Arts Council pleaded neutrality but its communications were adrift. It had no long-term drama representative. *However,* the Chairman, Dr T Webster, made one of the few practical proposals of the day --a modest five-hundred seater theatre, just to kick off with. This suggestion was rejected as not being "up to the mark." The Trust's single, simple, almost desperate bid for a similar small theatre in Cardiff's Sophia Gardens, was also brushed aside.

A further sticky critic now appeared, Wilbert Lloyd-Roberts, spokesman for Welsh language drama. He rejected the idea of a Cardiff-based theatre. Cardiff, he believed, was inaccessible to the rest of Wales. It was, *moreover,* monoglot --a parvenue capital by Royal Appointment, created out of the 1957 Cardiff Commonwealth Games. Wilbert Lloyd Roberts favoured a travelling national theatre, although the currently touring Welsh Drama Company was no great argument for his case.

But Welsh-speaking opposition was itself divided. Saunders Lewis, Wales's leading Welsh-speaking dramatist, did come out for a Cardiff-based theatre, believing that professionalism had to come before language. But Saunders Lewis, like the Trust, went overboard and he visualized a theatre instantly "on a par with the best in London, Paris or Moscow." A further irony lay in the fact that many members of the Trust were themselves Welsh speaking.

As the dialogue, in both languages, became brisker, yet another theatre champion appeared, His Worship The Lord Mayor of Cardiff, Alderman Lincoln Halinan. In 1969, the City Council had acquired the lease on Cardiff's one-thousand seater New Theatre. Mayor

Halinan therefore felt himself qualified to dismiss Dr Webster's mini five-hundred seater as "mean, parochial and unimaginative." Civic pride had now taken the stage. It made Wales's Great Seating Capacity Debate even murkier and more venomous.

Alun Richards "gave up writing plays"

In the late sixties, the various intrigues came to a nasty head. The floundering Welsh Drama Company registered itself as the Welsh **National** theatre. This provoked wrath of biblical dimensions. Had not the St David's Trust copyrighted the treasured "National"? It was the Trust alone which was in possession of the sacred word! Gauntlets were thrown down; seconds exchanged cards; writs were issued. However, this astonishingly vitriolic row was settled out of court and the Welsh Drama Company was forced to drop the hot-potato "National" from its title.

In the early seventies, the Trust borrowed a prestigious new Lord, Lord Chalfont, as its next Chairman. This final, futile piece of bureaucratic snobbery failed. The St David's Trust was at its last gasp. Its penultimate scheme in 1974, still, incredibly, opted for a national theatre of mammoth proportions. This last bid was made at a time when an ambitious new theatre-building programme was nearing completion and the new civic and collegiate theatres soon succeeded where the Trust had so signally failed --they actually got themselves built. Wales now suddenly had not one but at least four theatres which could be termed "national" --at least, in size. By the mid-seventies, the Trust had lost all relevance and credibility and it voluntarily wound up its activities.

But what of the third Big Body in all this --the Welsh Committee of the Arts Council of Great Britain? In 1967, Whitehall decided on autonomy and the WCAC became independent as the Welsh Arts Council. Its failure in terms of drama was immediate and total. During the period of the early bitter controversies, 1967-

70, the Welsh Arts Council had somehow overlooked the obvious necessity of appointing a drama officer. When it did, in 1970, it selected a non-Welshman with no knowledge of Wales, and little understanding of the recent diplomatic flurries. In spite of this, the Welsh Arts Council was presented with a rare and undeserved opportunity. The directorship of the Welsh Drama Company fell vacant. Could anything be done to salvage the sad remnants of Welsh national theatre projects? The Welsh Arts Council proceeded to destroy the last vestiges of hope at a single stroke. It appointed the Director of the Welsh National Opera Company to the Directorship of the Welsh Drama Company. Michael Geliot, an Englishman, now became both commissar of Welsh drama **and** opera. This obtuse and volatile mix promised disaster. It was not long in coming.

The Welsh Drama Company was still without a main stage. Michael Geliot with the backing of the Welsh Arts Council, decided that the new collegiate Sherman Theatre in Cardiff (opened in 1973) would be just the place for his forlorn troupe of Welsh barn-players. But differences of opinion now broke out between Michael Geliot and the Sherman's new benign English Director, Geoffrey Axworthy. Anglo-Saxon hostilities compounded the already confused state of inter-Celtic theatre feuds. These public multi-national bickerings were an endearing feature of the English theatre in Wales in the mid- and late seventies.

In 1975, The Welsh arts Council was offered a further unexpected chance. Its post of Drama Director became available. Would there be a new broom? Would a sane plan or policy emerge? Everything depended on the candidate selected. This turned out to be the outgoing English Drama Director's administrative assistant.

Fresh crises were soon brewing. They culminated in 1978 with the messy, high-handed "removal" of Michael Geliot from his dual role in Welsh drama and opera. His even messier "reinstatement" sometime later, did little to elevate the official image of drama in Wales.

But there was at least one definite false note. After the "now you see him, now you don't!" game with Michael Geliot, the Welsh Drama Company ceased to be seen at all. Thus, another contender in the bruising combat came to a sour and sticky end. The real victim in all this squalor was, of course, the dream of a Welsh national theatre. The bemused public, who was to have paid for it all, was, by this time, over the hills and far away, bored to extinction.

What would the new collegiate and civic theatres do? Would they pick up the Standard? In a few short seasons, they became, without exception, uncanny look-alikes of the defunct Welsh Drama Company --sluggish imitations of the most moribund of English provincial Rep companies. The playwrights, whose work represents the only real, lasting achievements of the sixties and seventies, found no home, hope or comfort in them. Welsh actors resigned themselves to part-time jobs in Wales and permanent addresses in England.

The continuing crises in the theatre in Wales during the thirty year period 1950-80, stand as a permanent indictment of official ineptitude, waste and ignorance. It also stands as a warning to the vanity of all future plans and planners. Yet the agonizing hope lingers on - a truly Welsh National Theatre could still come into being if common sense and passion were given but half a chance to work.

P M Margareth Thatcher
Graciously responded to questions on Welsh Drama

# Welsh Theatre post-war Hopes to the Disasters of the Seventies

In 1953 *Under Milk Wood* was given its premiere in New York. In 1956, the year of *Look Back in Anger,* it was first staged in London. This "play for voices" gave the theatre of the fifties one of its most endearing classics. But Welsh theatre was not all *Milkwood.*

Emlyn Williams, the link between pre-war and post-war theatre- writing, was also busy and his *Someone Waiting* was produced in 1953. Another "old wave" writer was performed, too;twenty-six years after its London success, BBC Wales broadcast a radio adaptation of Richard Hughes's *A Comedy of Good and Evil.* Outraged Welsh theologians denounced it as "unchristian" and it has not been heard of since. (Such a play could of course be tolerated, but only outside Wales).

New triumphs there were --but necessarily all in London. Alun Owen's *Progress to the Park* and *The Rough and Ready Lot* were first seen there in 1959 and other plays of his were regularly produced in the sixties. The Royal Court first produced Gwyn Thomas's *The Keep* (1961). Further plays followed in 1962 and 1963. The Belgrade, Coventry, introduced another Welsh dramatist, Alun Richards with *The Big Breaker (1965).* Richards continued with *The Victualler's Ball* (1969) and *The Snowdropper* took him into the seventies. In the sixties, Peter Gill's work was also first staged, with *A Collier's Friday Night* (1965), also at the Royal Court. Further plays followed in 1968 and 1969. *Small Change* (1976) established him in the seventies. Dannie Abse's first play *A House of Cowards* (1963) was produced at The Questors Theatre, Ealing. Premieres of further plays followed at the same theatre. Abse sustained his initial success with *The Dogs of Pavlov (1974)* and *Pythagoras* (1976) at the Birmingham Repertory Company.

**Footnote**
Dedwydd Jones's play BARD was recently named as the outstanding entrant in the International Living Playwright's Competition organized by Dragon's Teeth Press of Georgetown, California. It has also been sold to Radio-TV Suisse Romande. He has three one-act plays currently being published in the U.S.A.

Theatre Clwyd's *My People* adapted and directed by Gareth Jones

## Continuing Successes

Wales's contribution to the UK theatre, apart from internationally known actors such as Stanley Baker and Richard Burton, was therefore both continuing and considerable. But these achievements were all made outside of Wales. Why? The plea in the fifties and sixties was that there were "no theatres" in Wales, and indeed there **were** only the Cardiff New and the Swansea Grand to represent "Welsh" theatre --such as it was. There was also the Welsh Drama Company (WDC) founded in 1962, but it was, and remained until its demise, a company without a main stage. Its first director, Warren Jenkins, attempted to give the company a "regional" emphasis, but between 1962 and 1965 only four out of the eighteen main productions were by Welsh authors. Without an adequate theatre, the WDC had perforce to improvise on a dozen hired stages, until Warren Jenkins finally resigned in despair. After his departure, the WDC went on from weakness to weakness, until its bankruptcy and threatened dissolution today (1978). Meanwhile the new wave writers like Gwyn Thomas and Alun Richards, although now well established as dramatists, are still forced to seek their premières out of Wales.

By the seventies, Welsh theatre had two sources of material to draw on --the Caradoc Evans-Richard Hughes body of plays, and those of the new wave writers. How have these two generations of Welsh writers fared in the seventies? And how have our theatres used them?

In the late sixties, new theatres were planned at Cardiff, Aberystwyth, Mold, Milford, Bangor and

Builth. By the mid-seventies, concrete monuments of hideous expense had sprung up - the subsidized theatre had come into its own. The (University) Sherman Theatre opened with. *The Government Inspector* (1973) by Gogol --the Russian Caradoc Evans! The play was directed by Michael Geliot, newly appointed Artistic Director of the Welsh Drama Company (WDC). Geliot was also at the same time, Artistic Director of the Welsh National Opera Company --the sort of one-man monopoly beloved of socialist Wales. Thereafter, the Sherman went on from strength to strength, and it is now Wales's most prestigious film theatre. Something, too, happened at the WDC. Between 1973 and 1977, twenty-three main stage productions were seen. However, only three of these were by Welsh writers, including Geliot's astonishing premiere of Gwyn Thomas's Sap. Meanwhile Aberystwyth's cavernous new University Theatre echoed to empty hopes and emptier auditoriums. Swansea Grand pressed on with its thirties hits from Shaftesbury Avenue. Milford's new Torch Theatre opened in November 1977 with a "documentary" on the Victor of Trafalgar, the diminutive Norfolk Admiral (born 1758). The WDC, after recent acrimonious staff "rationalisations", now boasts yet another Artistic Director and yet another policy. The last months of 1977 saw *Tales from Chaucer* (died circa 1390) and adaptations from Holmes (Sherlock). 1978 was ushered in with a Jubilee sing-along based on the work of jolly imperialist, Rudyard Kipling --all in the Year of Devolution. However, it is the new Mold Theatre that most typifies the fate of Welsh drama in the seventies. The theatre lists 28 plays since it opened in 1976. Here are the Mold play results:

English plays :16
Irish plays :3 (two by same author)
American plays: 3
German plays: 1
Hungarian "Fro licks": 1
Pantos: 2
Old play by Emlyn Williams 1
Translation and adaptation from a novel in Welsh: 1.
Final score: Other plays 27; Welsh plays 1.

The average age of the plays (from date of writing) is 144 years - encouraging news for all 144-year-old playwrights- but only non-Welsh ones. Most of the twenty-eight plays listed above were also on the local "0" and "A" level set text lists, boring fare, therefore, for all 144 -year-old theatre-goers who had already passed their exams.

The Mold theatre is also hosting a "Welsh" playwriting competition, organized by the Liverpool Daily Post, in England! - hence the theatre's proud claim that it "relates to the communities of North Wales."

But there were attempts to initiate a new drama. There was, for example, the Welsh Artists' Workshop (WAW), founded in 1969 by actor Ray Smith and writers Bill Meilen and Dedwydd Jones. Their aim was to provide a platform for the work of Welsh writers and actors. The emphasis was strongly on the actor-manager - writer tradition. Ready support came from individual enthusiasts, which included cheques from Richard Burton and Elizabeth Taylor. In November 1969, WAW opened at the Cardiff New Theatre with a short run of two plays by native playwrights. However, it was precisely at this time that Wales was granted its own autonomous "Welsh" Arts Council. WAW, with its disreputable "bohemian" actor-writer image, was finally trampled to death in the stampede of the new "respectable" White Elephant subsidized theatres, for more and still more funds.

Emlyn Williams as Charles Dickens

The lines in the 1970's were therefore clearly drawn between the indigene-writer-actor-managers on one hand, and the new subsidized theatres, with their bureaucratic placemen, the Artistic Directors, on the other.

In spite of the big battalions, solitary individuals still had a go. Actor Michael Forrest toured the neglected valley halls in 1971 with an independent production of, splendidly enough, *The Duchess of Malfi*. The venture aroused enthusiastic local support but none at the centre --Museum Place, the appropriately named home of the new WAC. Michael Forrest went on to stage Wales's first home-grown rock musical *Tom Jones Slept Here* (1974), adapted from the novel by Pontypridd author RL Hughes. This second project was also well-received locally, but after an irreverant, exciting one-week run, it encountered official disapproval and foundered, due mainly to abrupt financial under-nourishment.

But more lasting, independent success did come. Martin Williams took over as Manager of the Cardiff New, a theatre well outside the new WAC theatre-subsidized orbit. In a few years. The New was prospering, both artistically and financially. By 1976, Martin Williams with a judicious mixture of old and new plays, pantos and classics, had proved that shows **could** pay. His death at thirty two, robbed Wales of one of its very few real managerial and professional hopes.

These varied and distinctive achievements were the result of individual effort and individual enterprise. The success of the new fringe groups, too, showed all the vigour and imagination which the main stages so conspicuously lacked. Pryderi and his Pigs, Theatre Yr

Ymylon and the excellent work of the Chapter Arts Centre, Cardiff, for example were founded by individuals and flourished under individuals. Unhappily, they succeeded in thoroughly alarming the new rich officialdom, and suspicion of individual talent became endemic. This neglect was striking, especially if the individual happened to be an actor, a writer or Welsh. If he was all three, then he was virtually untouchable.

Wales, too, "is a sow that devours her own farrow", where the sow "Establishment" lives in terror of its own offspring. All the main theatres of Wales, for example, are, without exception, controlled by non-Welshmen. The majority of the fringe groups even, are out of Welsh hands. The WAC's Drama Officer 44 between 1970 and 1976 was a stranger to Wales and to Welsh oddities. Welsh theatre grants and bursaries therefore necessarily ignore Welsh needs. The main "theatre bursaries" of 1976-77, went mostly to dancers, designers and administrators, largely non-Welsh. 1977's single "theatre bursary" for a writer went to English poet James Kirkup, (at the Sherman). 1976 and 1977's most useless awards were to France's Eugene Ionesco and Switzerland's Fred Durrenmatt (£1,000 each), plus translations, productions and tours of their work. Wales is very much a nation of quirky folk, with peculiarities of language both in the English and the Welsh tongue, and it needs its own lunatics to direct its own bizarre schemes in its own peculiar way. And why not? Every other country gives preference to its own home-grown idiots, geniuses and tomfooleries.

And what **is** the result of this deadly compound of fear of native talent and exclusion of originality? Bill

Meilen (WAW) and Michael Forrest, emigrated to Canada. Ray Smith went on to further successes - in fair Albion, as usual. Pryderi and his Pigs went on to hits, too - in America. Dannie Abse commented, "If I had been given one ounce of encouragement, I would have written more for Wales." Alun Richards declared, "I have given up writing plays." Gwyn Thomas remains speechless on the subject.

The twenties, thirties, forties, fifties and sixties all saw new and exciting contributions to British drama from Welshmen. The seventies however are so bare of fresh writing talent that there is now no Welsh dramatist under the age of forty. If the end product of drama is plays, then it must be said that at the moment there is no worthwhile drama in Wales at all.

### Buried Talent

The situation is summed up in a series of vivid metaphors by Raymond Edwards, Principal of the Welsh College of Music and Drama, "Streams of talent with no reservoir; a wheel with many spokes but no hub; a vineyard where the quality of the wine is untested; tanks with nothing to put in them." And, most telling of all, "If Wales was represented in the parable of the talents, it would be by the third son, who buried his."

In artistic terms, therefore, the subsidized theatre experiment in Wales has been an unequivocal disaster, and it is the largest subsidies and the largest stages which are directly responsible for the present debacle. Wales's subsidized theatres have become Houses of the

Dead in which the ghosts of the Welsh past are doubly doomed.

The seventies have been the meeting point of disasters. Talk of dinosaurs (see The Stage, February 26th,1976), is now, at last, out in the open. The Western Mail (December 12th,1977) stated that "our main theatres have assumed the blank stares of white elephants." The article further emphasizes the financial as well as the artistic bankruptcy of the subsidized theatres. The new Torch Theatre at Milford is still a quarter of a million pounds in debt. Theatre Gwynedd (Bangor) is £50,000 in the red. The Mold Theatre has to pay over £100,000 in loan interests to survive; the new Artistic Director is already threatening resignation. Meanwhile the exciting fringe groups have to limp along. The entire annual drama budget, for example, of the Chapter Arts Centre is £8,000.

But the disaster has assumed even wider proportions. The Welsh Arts Council itself is under close official scrutiny, due to "rising tides of criticism" (Western Mail, December 15th, 1977). During the 1977 Welsh Grand Committee Debate on the Arts, Emlyn Hooson, Liberal MP for Montgomeryshire, called for an open conference on the functioning of the Arts Council. The conference will take place in July or October of this year (1978) - "outside Cardiff"-- to allay fears that the event "would be dominated by Arts Council officials." On the Arts Council side there is fine talk of "public accountability" and "stewardship" but on the humble drama level, it is hard even to raise a mess of cold potage. On being asked about the plight of Welsh dramatists, the official answer came, "We are setting up a committee to look into just that." Asked whether such committees operated on a quorum, the reply was, "No!" It is this arrangement, of course, that gives rise to those annual free-for-alls, politely called "awards, bursaries and grants" by the WAC.

No quorums, no long-term plans, no policies, no coordination, no imagination, no accountability, no professionalism, no money - these are some of the deficiencies which must be publicly challenged, examined and corrected. Out of the disasters of the seventies must come reform, for without reform, there can be no future.

### Preference for Welsh

What should be done? Firstly, there must be a major shift away from the gigantic parasitic weeds which the subsidized theatres have become, to smaller groups, more modest theatres, and to individual enterprise. The main theatres must now be treated as ruthlessly as they have treated drama itself. They have not delivered the goods, artistically or financially. If, as the Western Mail states "fewer performances" is to be the result of these failures, then all very well. Let the failures go completely by the board, and the money be given over to smaller ventures like Chapter Arts Centre, which **has** delivered the goods on a minimum budget, but with maximum effect. Secondly, preference must be given to Welsh artists in Wales, from Artistic Directors all the way up to carpenters. Wales is unique in that it denies itself that most basic of all rights, the right to fail. In artistic terms, the move must be towards the writer-actor-manager tradition, keeping Martin Williams's work well in mind. In terms of writing for the theatre,

GB Shaw's 1914 article remains a permanent blueprint. The plays of the old wave and the new wave writers must be presented, for it is only by the promise of performance that new writing will emerge.

If, therefore, the emphasis is on reform, 1978 might well witness a re-birth of Welsh drama, however bedraggled the Phoenix, however battered its champions, and our "streams of talent" and "faculty of imagination" be seen, at long last, in all their richness, from Wales to the world.

The Stage, March 1978

# The Great Welsh Drama Controversy

## A Review the Theatre in Wales during 1978

Swansea Grand Theatre, the most elegant in Wales

Philipp Madoc, of Theatre Wales Company, as Lloyd George

In 1978, the Welsh Theatre presented its usual inchoate image. Its keynote was extreme oddness. The celebrations of the Great Dead Man of Wales, Dylan Thomas, saw some unlovely excesses, while the Welsh Arts Council (WAC) staged its premiere "Public Forum," a bizarre mixture of farce, philistinism and paper-hanging.

But, first, Dylan. His *Under Milkwood* advanced from Laugharne, Dyfed, towards the White House, USA, via invitations to 10 Downing St, corners in the Abbey, Milkwood Art Competitions in The Observer Supplement, "win a weekend for two in Dylanland" in the Western Mail, commemorative labels in the Post Office, all the way to the Mayfair Theatre, London. Here, a so-called "Welsh National Theatre" celebrated the Great Dead Man in gala performance. Most peculiar. This group, the Welsh speaking section of the half-dead Welsh Drama Company (WDC), should, by definition and duty, be performing plays in Welsh to Welsh-speaking audiences in Wales. They receive £170,000 p.a. to do just that.

No "Welsh National Theatre" legally exists. However, perhaps to make good this lack, a Dylan Thomas Memorial Theatre project was announced. In Swansea's old dockland, a disused garage known as "the Old Chess Building" will be converted. Not far away, the Dylan Bookshop in Swansea's Salubrious Passage is already well-known. A further unlikely champion of Welsh drama also arose in 1978 –the Presbyterian Church of Wales! It, too, outlined its own unique scheme. One of the Church's empty chapels in Cardiff will be converted into a theatre for Theatr Yr Ymylon.

However, all "sexromp, bad taste and low-repute plays" have been banned in advance, along with the sale of alcohol. The driest drama experience in the U.K. awaits theatre-lovers at Wales's sainted theatre of Presbyters. Meanwhile, down the road, the magnificent old Prince of Wales Theatre will be rebuilt into "a luxury entertainment centre" specializing "in one night stands."

While these striking new ventures were coming into being, the WAC was winding up an old one. The WDC (English-speaking section) founded in 1962, headed by Michael Geliot, ceased to exist. £30,000 was spent on paying off its personnel. Simultaneously, Geliot was "removed" from the direction of the Welsh National Opera Company. Geliot, the Company and Equity strenuously objected, and Geliot was reinstated --but only in song. His present, ingenious, title - "artistic Consultant and Principal Producer" to the Welsh National Opera. The truncated Welsh-speaking half of the WDC ended up at the English speaking Mayfair Theatre - odd bed-fellows bach!

Cardiff's Sherman Theatre celebrated its fifth anniversary with a "massive variety" of culture, including a talk "on the ideas behind the Sherman" - a preliminary, no doubt, to the Parade of the Primadonnas which followed. The Sherman's Director, Geoffrey Axworthy, rejected the idea of developing an indigenous Welsh Theatre Company on the grounds that it would become "elitist" and "monopolist." The Sherman, he argued, had no need to stick to a formula, "We have an opportunist kind of programme which picks up what is in the air." (Western Mail, October 22nd,1978.) The re-instated Mr Geliot promptly i?-accused Mr Axworthy of

"a grave disservice to the professional theatre in Wales."
He cited the Sherman's "dismal" attendance figures and
accused the WAC of being "gullible" in accepting them.
He described Mr Axworthy's prose as"euphoric" and his
overall performance as "pretty appalling",(Western
Mail, October 12th,1978). "Distorted... obsessed...
unable to grasp wider purposes... boring," replied Mr
Axworthy, and returned to his film programmes. Mr
Geliot flew off to the Teatro Colon, Buenos Aires, to
produce Dido and Aeneas, just missing his operatic
colleague, Richard Armstrong, fresh from
Czechoslovakia, where he had been awarded a medal
for promoting the operas of Janacek in Wales. Messrs
Geliot and Axworthy are **not** native to Wales. Between
them they control £766,000 in subsidies from the WAC.

At the same time, the highly professional Cardiff-
born Laboratory Theatre, had struck a fine, if unusual,
balance. This Company "has a romance with Europe",
(Western Mail, August 14th). It annually tours the
Continent "to be sure of acclaim" and "to raise the
money necessary to pursue its aims in Wales." Due to its
overseas success, the WAC magnanimously raised the
theatre's subsidy so its actors actually received forty-five
pounds a week. Up in the north, the Mold Theatre
continued its irrelevant liaison with foreign novelists.
The adaptation of Jules Verne's *Journey to the Centre of
the Earth* warned of "actors climbing around the roof.
As from tomorrow!" The Torch Theatre, Milford Haven,
fell out of debt at last, but was immediately in the red
again, to the exasperation of local councillors. The
Torch celebrated with *Murder in the Red 8arn.* Wales's
principal theatres have now come to resemble ingrowing

toe-nails - they engender their own poisons and each is separately owned.

But the boob of the year goes to the Welsh Arts Council – which misplaced a theatre. In its annual report, a photograph carried the caption, "Theatre Gwynedd, Caernarvon." Theatre Gwynedd is, of course, in another town --Bangor-- miles up the road. The WAC's (drama) report further revealed it had spent £1,025,192 on promoting much of the above, but out of this massive total, only £13,525 went directly to individuals in the theatre. A breakdown of this figure reveals some singular features. Fees for professional tutors at the Welsh Youth Theatre, and grants to puppeteers, amounted to £2,100. £5,700 went to postgraduate students at the Welsh College of Music and Drama, to "study drama through the medium of Welsh." £200 also went on theatre administrators to learn Welsh. For example, the non-Welsh-speaking Director of the £55,000 p.a. Theatre Yr Ymylon, was paid the queer sum of seventy pounds to learn the language. The former Welsh-speaking director of the theatre, David Lynn, had been forced to resign a year earlier due to an inadequate salary level. A further five-hundred pounds went on the (Welsh-speaking) Eisteddfod drama prize. But perhaps all this is in line witli some twilight avant-garde theatre of Welsh learners that Wales is only just becoming aware of. The. dramatists themselves received a total of £2,450, mostly for adaptations and children's plays. Only one award went for an original work, five-hundred pounds for JL Hughes's *Shifts*. £500 out of a total of £1,025; 192 represents a percentage of 0.049. This aberrant figure is made all the more freakish by the huge success of the anniversary *Milkwood* –the original work, after all, of one solitary professional Welshman. A further despairing irony was added to 1978's unbalanced theatre image by the West Glamorgan County Council's own report on the Redcliffe-Maude Report on the Arts in Wales. The County Council observed, "The lack of structure has resulted in a watering down of expertise." It concluded, "The area is significantly lacking in professional practicing artists."

**Sham**

The WAC's Public Forum in September was false, farcical and autocratic. It was held in a town in Mid-Wales, well away from the main centres of population, in library premises of limited seating capacity; entry was by ticket, on application to --the WAC! Only forty-five minutes was allowed for each subject (drama, for example). The WAC's Chairpersoness, The Marchioness of Anglesey, exercised a veto on questions. The Forum was all part of the WAC's paper-promises of "democratisation" --in imitation, possibly, of the London Arts Council's recent soul-searchings. Proceedings were, nevertheless, quite brisk. The WAC was accused of being "middle-class", "centralist", "favouritist", "Welsh-speaking" and "beyond the control of anyone." (Western Mail, September 25th.) Mr Geliot berated the Marchioness for "cutting off his salary," something "he could not do to her."'

Mr Geliot added that he would prefer to see Mrs Thatcher running the Welsh Arts Council, for she, at least was answerable to a public. An enraged Mr Neil ap

Siencyn proclaimed, "The hand of the WAC is the kiss of death!" Professor Lewis Jones, for the WAC, denounced such detractors with merciless precision: "Three-quarters of what you say is misleading. A quarter is untrue and one-third is libellous!" The Artists' Representative, Mr David Petersen, afterwards commented, "We made no headway... the answers were *evasive...* we obtained no discussion on the fundamental point, the composition of the subject committees." Even the Western Mail called it "a public relations exercise." The director of the WAC promptly threatened further such forums.

It cannot be too strongly emphasized that the Welsh Arts Council in Wales is a monopoly. There is no alternative grant-making body. The WAC has, too, reportedly eschewed "the dead hand of professionalism." Its present structure makes it a "mediocracy" --an ugly marriage of amateurism and monopoly. Nowhere is this more evident than in the WAC's baleful and pernicious Bursaries System. To qualify for a bursary, a Welshman has to be resident in Wales, and resident for *twelve* months prior to application; he must also *give* up his job and produce evidence of this fact; he must also *have* been already published before applying in the first place. These conditions are deliberately designed to promote cliques and coteries by a *very* obvious system of universal disqualification depending on the whim of tile awarding body, and on the "good behaviour" of the applicant. This is, in reality, a Pauper's Charter, and it is at the very root of the antagonism which exists between the WAC and the artists. Equally disturbing is the WAC's annual award to foreign writers. This year, £1,000 went to the Danish children's writer, Astrid Lindgren, a reputed million heiress. Such bewildering profligacies must cease, if only to obviate junketings on the part of WAC officers and to curtail overseas displays of parochial Welsh vanity which can only bring Wales into contempt and ridicule. However, criticism of the WAC's "undemocratic" structure exists even in the WAC itself. The intrepid County Councillor, Mr Frank Evans, a member of the Drama Committee, has pointed out that as a County Councillor, he is the only democratically elected member of the Panel. Mr Evans, too, has suggested that half of the WAC's total of over three million in subsidies, should be "decentralised" to the Regional Arts Associations. Mr Evans has also argued that at least one third of the WAC's officers should be nominated from the (projected) Welsh Assembly. But, in spite of its posturings about "public accountability" etc, the WAC rejected all "interference" from the Assembly, a body, it is to be noted, that does not yet exist, (the Western Mail, November 6th).

**A Plan for Wales**

It is evident that the Arts in Wales require the application of a plan, and such a plan, for drama, was presented to the WAC and to other interested parties, by this writer during 1978. In part, the plan proposed the formation of an Office of Information, Coordination and Employment, for Welsh theatres and theatre artists. The aim was to eliminate the present Errors, Hostilities and Waste, and to promote a rational indigenous drama movement. The Plan further suggested that the appointment of dramatists be put on a par with directors, and that both should be made "accountable", on a contractual basis of three years. Any failure at the end of this period would result in termination of contract. It was pointed out that this arrangement would eliminate those distasteful public theatre rows so distressing to everyone in Wales.

Another section of the Plan proposed specific seasons of plays by Welshmen, including the old guard, (Richard Hughes, Caradoc Evans) and contemporary dramatists (Peter Gill, Dannie Abse) --these seasons to be run in conjunction with a playwriting 90mpetition to be held open for two years. Thereafter, a further season to consist of new plays by any Welshmen, new plays from the open competition, until such seasons finally achieved Granville-8arker's classic formula of one-third new plays, one-third established plays and one-third "foreign" drama.

Responses to this elementary plan were revealing. The WAC courteously read it "with interest and not a little irritation" and looked forward to further "talks." Dannie Abse believed that the theatre in Wales was "pathetic and autocratic" as well as rude to Welsh writers. Peter Gill had "nothing constructive to say." Jon Holliday (journalist) remarked, "Such a concentrated attempt has much to recommend it." He also advised this writer to be more polite. The Sunday Telegraph Supplement considered it "an interesting and invigorating plan." Dafydd Wigley, M.P., "I hope it will have started many minds thinking." Councillor Frank Evans, "The consumers of the Arts should have more say... I keep sniping... " David Lynn, founder and former director of Theatre Yr Ymylon, declared: "I like it all.. it makes me feel good that there are others who care. I feel as if I was shouting in the wilderness... your statement is reassuring." Mr Lynn, too, had presented his own plan in 1977, for a theatre "which would give expression to national identity." He was, thereafter, constrained to resign due to depressed salary conditions.

The reaction that sums up the attitude of the main theatres in Wales, came from the imperious Torch Theatre, Milford Haven: "You state your Plan is based on continuity, direction, logic and nationality. I detect little of these. It (the Plan) is so out of date ....so passe .... it does not merit serious thought... it was formed in a different era of Welsh theatre... We who live and work here always welcome helpful suggestions because we feel deeply about the development of drama, firstly in Wales, and, secondly, globally." The remaining White Elephant theatres ventured "no comment." The Torch, the Sherman, the Swansea Grand and Clwyd theatres, all run by non-Welshmen, enjoy subsidies of over £200,000 between them.

However, it is precisely these very obscurantist, mandarin, and essentially self-destructive attitudes, that have at last provoked the furious and radical opposition of the artists, the politicians, and, finally, the public. Most unfortunately of all, the WAC itself, by its failure to fulfil promises of reform and by public exhibitions of its most devastating shortcomings, has now impelled the future of the Arts in Wales into the political arena. As has already been officially suggested, the WAC's monopoly can now only be broken by a Welsh Assembly wielding wider and more democratic powers.

Unhappily, the establishment of a truly Welsh National Theatre now seems to depend on the results of the St. David's Day referendum. But whatever the outcome, matters and monopolies in the Arts in Wales can never again be the same. The referendum itself signals a gigantic change and the WAC must learn to recognise this. Meanwhile, though somewhat tattered, the artists wait in the wings, taking notes, making certain that events will be recorded as they happen. 1979 promises sea-changes as rich and strange as any of 1978's sad and maddening oddities.

The Stage, March 1979

# The Malaise of the Welsh Theatre
## A Review of the Theatre in Wales during 1979

The last year of the decade was the year of all the nations, except Wales.

At the Sherman we had *Springbok* by South African Michael Picardie; *Bix, Hoagy and... Bunkhouse* by Liverpool's Adrian Mitchell, and *Forever Yours, Mary Lou,* by Quebecois Michel Tremblay --to show Wales "life under two cultures."

*The* USA's New World Theatre toured *Metamorphoses.* The International Festival of Young People (Sherman again) imported groups from (among others) Sri Lanka, East Anglia, Hungary and Italy. The lone Welsh group went unlisted in the publicity blurbs. The Festival was organised by Bolton's own Robin Howarth.

Hungarian director George Roman (Mold) tripped to Budapest and returned with dramatist Ferenc Karinthy and his play *Stein way Grand.* Cardiff's Laboratory Theatre became distributors for "Italian-born Danish-based" writer, Eugenio Barba. Colin Wilson's *Mysteries* was commissioned by the Red Light Theatre. Cardiff's New Theatre confirmed its policy of "no home-produced plays" and we saw, instead, *Shut Your Eyes and Think of England.* Aberystwyth witnessed *The Englishman Amused* and *From the Greek* by F. Raphael, (the Cambridge Theatre Company).

Local productions were of the usual "0" level and Shaftesbury Avenue variety. Mold presented "a £44,000 double-bill", Shaw's *Caesar and Cleopatra* and Shakespeare's *Anthony and Cleopatra,* set in trendy 1910. The Torch (Milford Haven) simultaneously staged *Arms and the Man.*

However, the Welsh standard was kept flying by Cardiff's Children's Theatre, which presented Wales's national hero *Owain Glyndwr* directly after *The Owl and the Pussycat.* The Torch offered *Dragon's Galore,* also strictly for kids. As a leap forward, Gwyn Thomas's *The Keep* (1962) was revived and his *Testimonials* (from old material) premièred. To display Welsh bias, John McGrath of the visiting 7:84 Company was conferred with the sobriquet "Mold-born." However, the first-rate Chapter Arts Centre continued its clearly defined community role and staged *Terraces* by Alan Osborne, an entertainment based "on any typical Welsh iron town." The adventurous Open Cast Company premièred *The Battle of the Rock,* a documentary on the great anthracite mine strike of 1925. But apart from these rare exceptions, Wales's 1979-80 playbills were as doomed and stodgy as those established by the (now dead) Welsh Drama Company as far back as 1962.

### Bleak

The gloomy seventies closed to lots of "bleak futures", while "closure threats" "cash crises" and "theatre rows" abounded. Wales's sweet, sad, mysterious Theatre of Prebyters folded completely. After two theatres has refused to underwrite its somewhat inchoate tours (Western Mail, October 3rd, 1979), South African-born director Norman Florence "ceased trading" due to a "cash crisis" although £42,000 still remained of the Presbyters sweet annual grant of £90,000.

The still intrepid WAC drama member, Frank (Democratically Elected) Evans, accused the Llandovery Theatre of being "elitist and exclusive," which it is. But so what? All of Wales's main theatres are run on these principles - or rather lack of them.

Meanwhile, the Torch's director fell on Amoco, claiming that the oil company's gift of £250,000 to the Welsh National Opera was also "elitist." The director went on to "slam" the Welsh Arts Council, which had cut its grant from a promised £90,000 to a measly £70,000. But all unheeding, Amoco's lorries continue to rumble past the Torch's troubled doors and the theatre still faces possible extinction.

But it was Mold's bold administrator, Roger Tomlinson, who really took up cudgels for weedy Wales. He belaboured Westminster in choice language: "Wales has been shortchanged. This means loss of jobs. The increase is only 11.8 per cent."

After this broadside, he returned to organise Mold's modest £44,0000 double-bill. But harassed Mold has need of dashing administrators. It enjoys the largest WAC subsidy in Wales (£120,000) as well as lavish local grants (1979-80 --£339,870). Mold's lead was soon taken up by the WAC itself, and, it, too, lambasted London. "This leads to a crisis in the theatre. Wales has a living language." But there is no job shortage in the WAC's drama department. It now has a Drama Officer, a Drama and Dance Officer, a Second Drama Officer, an Administrative Assistant and a Secretary. It also generously offered a "Publicity and Promotions Bursary" to its own officers at the height of the cuts.

An overpowering odour came over the WAC's Writers Awards System. After severe criticsm (The Stage, March, 1979 and the Western Mail, March 14th, 1979) the Director of Literature suspended all bursaries to writers. This, it was stated, was due solely to "a lack of cash."

However, the shortage was not so acute that it affected Wales's loopy International Writer's Award. This usually goes to needy overseas literary best-sellers but in 1979 it went to poor (but sunny) Trinidad. Caribbean poet-dramatist Derek Walcott collects the £1,000 prize. This year he will enjoy an all expenses-paid trip to Wales - pour encourager les scribes gallois - no doubt, and, of course, to teach them to keep their mouths shut.


### Aspirations

The healthiest theatre developments had little to do with the WAC's games of theatrical chance. The three-stage Llanelli theatre and the Wyeside Arts Center opened their doors, without benefit of WAC. Llanelli's theatre was converted from the old Odeon cinema at a cost to the local council of £340,000, at 1978 prices. A single new civic theatre was estimated at over a million pounds.

The Wyeside, too, was converted from an existing structure. It cost £150,000, not much more than the WAC's annual subsidy to its Mold white elephant. Both the Wyeside and the Llanelli theatres are the result of individual enterprise and imagination. They are rooted in their own communities and are run by locals for locals. They are not dependent on the poisoned and spasmodic largesse of the WAC.

The WAC's threatened Public Drama Forum went on and off, at the Sherman, (Western Mail, October 7th). The actors at once accused the WAC of being "a threat to their jobs." The evergreen Michael Geliot declared that the WAC, in the absence of a plan or policy, could no longer justify any increase in its annual subsidy. The Chairman of the Panel immediately promised a "document of aspirations." In its annual report, the WAC had already published a plan to promote Welsh play- writing, but this merely turned out to be the old system dyed pink. All applications for support from dramatists must still come via directors. But it is now doubtful whether the paper-tigers of the WAC can really shift the packs of placemen which now control our theatres. The Forum demonstrated that much more drastic surgery is needed.

The simple, over-all, end-of-decade message is clear. The subsidised theatre experiment in Wales is a disastrous flop. Our theatres have degenerated into free parking places for affluent tourists. Much of the money that comes from London eventually returns there by way of imported directors, actors, technicians, etc, and by outside touring companies. So little of

The money intended for Wales actually gets into Welsh pockets, the cash might as well stay in London in the first place. Mr Geliot's assertion that the WAC can no longer justify an increased subsidy is substantially accurate, as is the actors' claim that the WAC is "a threat to their jobs."

As matters now stand, the Minister for the Arts could safely axe a large part of the drama subsidy for all the difference it would make to Welsh theatre. The universal odium which attaches to the WAC at present, is, in itself, the most intractable obstacle of all.

The WAC's slavish dependence on outsiders must be finally curbed and its white elephants cut down to size. Only an immediate official inquiry into the WAC's entrenched twelve-year monopoly can now clear the way for progress or policy.

There is little doubt that if the WAC continues in its present form, the eighties will witness the same recriminations, futilities and waste that characterised so many of the sad Welsh drama debacles of the seventies.

The Stage, March 1980

# Welsh Drama and Dramatists

## A Review of the Theatre in Wales in 1980

1980 saw "the great Caradoc Evans" (died 1945) come back from the dead! And what a welcome we Welsh kept for the boyo: "A twisted talent... all malice... unnatural... makes us all witless idiots... venomous... A disappointed man with a twisted mind." (Letters to the Welsh Press, 1980).

But some reviewers differed, "Still disturbs... bites viciously... theatrical punch." (the Western Mail). "Tremendous fun. Very moving" (The Stage). "Ring of truth... completely convincing... " (The Guardian). "Time has not rusted Caradoc's blade" (Evening Leader).

At last, in an all-Welsh production, writer-producer Gareth Jones's superb adaptation of *My People* struck home. All praise to the Anglo-Hungarian bloc at Mold for hosting the play, albeit in its small studio theatre.

Five years ago in a St David's Day article for The Stage, I advocated the free use of Caradoc and other forgotten but potent Taffy remedies. Without *My People,* the Welsh Theatre invalid of 1980 would have expired.

The second saving event of 1980-1981 was Theatre Wales, with Ray Smith, Phillip Madoc, Hywel Bennett, Glyn Owen and friends, together for the first time in Wales in an all-Welsh venture. And, again, what a welcome was kept by our own Welsh Arts Council - a grudging £25,000 grant, but no promise, plan,

83

encouragement or theatre to make the group's future more assured. (The WAC, may, of course, be waiting for the reviews). So Theatre Wales's first production *What the Butler Saw* will be temporarily housed at the Sherman, Cardiff, for a precarious, one-off two-week run.

Meanwhile, the Western Mail revealed that the WAC had spent £340,000 of its £4.6 million grant on "administration" – that is, on itself. To calm outrage at these figures, the WAC had earlier set up a sub-committee costing £15,000 to make its costing "more efficient." Thereafter, the WAC was able to reassure its officers that there would be "no redundancies" but warned of "savings in telephone bills" (the Western Mail, December 3rd, 1980).

Rhymney Festival organisers, too, came out for the Welsh Leech Industry, spending £12,000 of its total of £23,000 Arts grant on "council" administrators. (The Stage, October 9th, 1980). To cool some of the heat, the WAC's Chairpersoness, Lady Anglesey, suggested "business and industrial sponsorship" and gratefully accepted a £5,000 handout from Gulf Oil for the Torch's production of Godspell at Milford.

The WAC went on to thump every Local Authority in Wales for failing to fund the arts adequately, comparing England's 46 per cent per person per annum to Wales's measly 26 percent per person per annum. To show what accountability really meant, the WAC then axed Swansea's exciting Open Cast Company, literally in mid-rehearsal. The Company berated the WAC for being "authoritarian and secretive." (The Stage, December, 1980). Even the conservative Western Mail expressed exasperation at the WAC's "hand to mouth" funding and demanded "a long-term strategy."

As usual, peculiarities and contradictions were everywhere. Carmarthen (Dyfed) decided on a £600,000 theatre, to be backed by the late Ben Travers. Bedwas, instead, appealed to common sense and converted its 1923 Workman's Hall into "the first grass roots theatre in the valley" at a fraction of the cost.

Then, weirdly, in the midst of all these openings and closings, cuts and squanderings, demands arose for **expanded** expenditure on imported drama.

Swansea's Festival organisers envisioned an "Edinburgh-style" international "fringe extravaganza." But the ever intrepid Councillor Evans called the Festival "elitist and stuffy."

Theatre Powys will present groups from Holland, France etc., during its Youth Theatre Festival. Mold's Director appealed for a scheme "to promote international exchanges." (The Stage, February 4th, 1980).

The Sherman's Director, Geoffrey Axworthy, spent "a workingholiday" at Edinburgh buying in shows for Cardiff's starving, grateful indigenes. The Sherman, now South Africa's leading theatre, threw in Welsh-prize-winning West-Indian dramatist, Derek Walcott. The Sherman's pet Czech, Dr Evzen Drmola, did Chekov's *Three Sisters.* Eugenio Barba and his Odin Teatret had a terrific "forum" there and Mgr. Carmen Jacobi directed Mrozek. Finally, Mike Picardie's *Jo'burgh Messiah* thrilled Tiger bay's army of unemployed.

All this, coming on top of the usual soggy acres of Brecht, Durrenmatt, etc, saw Wales's raw Elitist Controversy erupt once again. The 1980 outbreak was particularly virulent in Llandovery, where Director Simon (Taffs-under-the-Bed) Barnes, accused local Mahdis of inflicting "delays, ignorance, incompetence and bigotry" on him. Barnes had earlier celebrated a £25,000 EEC grant by staging *The Caretaker* with himself in the lead, hardly soothing medicine for the whirling dervishes of Llandovery. With glaring eye, he finally accused the local Welsh "of wanting to keep the local arts Welsh!" (The Stage, October 16th, 1980).

Meanwhile Wales's own actor-writer group, Theatre '81, failed to get bookings at any of the main theatres in Wales and folded. They bitterly accused Welsh theatres "of giving preference to companies from England." (the Western Mail October 9th,1980).

The Aberystwyth Arts Festival was also taken to task "for not reflecting Welsh talent" and Welsh Equity members demanded stronger representation in London.

The last word in contradiction, however, came from Mold's Roger Tomlinson, who denounced the Welsh press in a letter to the Welsh press (the Western Mail, October 3rd, 1980). He complained that "we" are "reported in a way that suggests that the arts are rather rarefied and elitist." It was this same press that gave Mold's *My People* wide coverage and praise.

Again to *My People,* the main theatre hit of 1980. Why had it taken Welsh Caradoc over half a century to first appear in Wales? Is the condition of dramatists there so benighted? Wesker recently declared the playwright "an endangered species." In 1972, in a letter to The Stage, I declared the Welsh dramatist to be an "extinct species" - but only in Wales! Why, then, is the dramatist extinct or threatened? Wesker squarely blames directors and their preference for "classics, improvisation and... collective writing." Well, why these preferences in the first place?

A look therefore at what directors in Wales said about new drama in 1980. Geoffrey Axworthy (Sherman) blamed the lack of new drama on his audiences, "They are conditioned only to see plays they know." (the Western Mail, December, 1979). Then he blamed "the unknown play --most difficult to sell." Then he slammed finance, "The squeeze will make it even more difficult for new plays!" (unless, of course, they are imported from South Africa). Mold's Tomlinson also indicted his audiences, "I want to broaden their tastes." (Letter to the Western Mail, April, 1980).

The Torch's director blamed literary history, "There has been no real growth in Welsh drama in the English language." (the Western Mail, April, 1980). Such twisted directorial fictions, however, have not gone unexamined.

Jean Kingdon (the Western Mail, December, 1980) suggested "a deeper malaise.. the public don't want to see the plays on offer." Robin' Lyons (the Western Mail, March, 1980) suggested that Mold's theatre was "easier game for encyclopaedia salesmen than for new writers." Mr Lyons concluded, "The most effective way for writers to ensure that their plays are performed is for them to do it themselves."

The last word must go to Roger Tomlinson, "If there is any new talent, it isn't knocking on our door!" (the Western Mail, March, 1980). - an open invitation, almost, for the cringing native dramatists to knock **down** the door to gain admittance to their own theatre in their own country.

Be it noted that in all of the above, the directors blamed everybody and everything except themselves. Wesker's strictures have proved justified. Directors, especially directors of subsidized theatres, direct only for themselves. "Classics" and "imports" represent no threat to them. But new drama does, for new drama would point up the sterility, the parasitism, the opportunism and the megalomania of this gruesome reign of directors. New drama would render the present role of the director redundant. This the directors know only too well and they fear it above all else. It is their vanity and cupidity alone that explains their total inability to recognize that in Working-Man Wales, their arrogance and insufferable air of superiority are absolutely detested.

There is no doubt that the radical *My People* and the new Theatre Wales Company stand as beacons in 1980-81 but it would be unrealistic to believe that such native successes are really welcome. It is certain that if 1981 does see any striking theatre successes in Wales, they will have nothing to do with the despicable and unnatural "director's theatre", 1963-1981, RIP!

The Stage, March 1981

**Footnote**

Dedwydd Jones's play BARD was recently named as the outstanding entrant in the International Living Playwright's Competition organized by Dragon's Teeth Press of Georgetown, California. It has also been sold to Radio-TV Suisse Romande. He has three one-act plays currently being published in the U.S.A.

68 Theatre Clwyd's *My People* adapted and directed by Gareth Jones

# Getting a Play On in Wales

During **81-1982**

1981-82 revealed that there were almost as many plays in Wales as there were Welshmen out of work. The Play for Wales Competition, for example, received over 155 entries. Bag and Baggage's much needed Practical Play Workshop brought in 60 pieces from 46 writers. The newly formed Welsh Dramatist's Network (WON) added up the unperformed plays of just three of its members - sixty two!

The fate of this tidy bundle of plays, especially the new entries for the Play for Wales Competition, was illuminating. No outright winner could be found among the 155 but three plays were singled out for commendation and prizes. The rest were returned without comment. However, neither the WAC nor any theatre in Wales had made provision for a possible production of any of the plays. The three "winning" dramatists were fobbed off with "rehearsed readings" and £500 was docked from their prize money to help pay for the readings. The dramatists were, of course, not consulted at any point. Mrs Sue Harries, the Competition's capable Organiser, thereafter resigned, outraged at the "slicing away" of the funds. Her £9,000 salary, she hoped, would be "made available for future literary activities."

Bag and Baggage which had successfully staged four new plays, had its entire subsidy slashed and went out of business. Its adventurous director, Christine Bradwell, returned to London. Dramatist Jonah Jones (twelve plays written in five years!) also decided "to go back to England." Roger Stennett with plays 69 produced at Hampstead, Brighton and Manchester, and dramatist Juliet Ace, also moved back over the border. As this stream of talent disappeared, the English-based Hull Truck Company moved in with *In Dreams,* a play "about Aberconwy." The 7.84 Company presented a musical "on life in the South Wales valleys."

The WAC continued to endorse its "Welsh not" policy with its ill-famed "International Award." £1,000 was again lost abroad to best-selling Canadian children's author, Margaret Atwood.

In the North, Mold's Budapest Theatre had its WAC grant raised from £140,000 to £157,000 and celebrated by going native. Exile Jeff Thomas's *Playing the Game* was imported from the Antipodes, "A palpable hit!" (the Wellington Post, New Zealand). Earlier, a Welsh "dramaturge" had even been appointed to Mold. Roger Tomlinson's baffling justification for this was "so few scripts were dropping through the letter box." And, "The simple fact is that there never has been a flow of scripts from potential playwrights." The dramaturge did finally discover a Welsh dramatist and the Wales was presented with – Emlyn Williams!

Three members of the Welsh Dramatist's Network duly checked known unperformed plays, including those submitted to Mold, and found that their original totals were absolutely correct. Hundreds of the little buggers everywhere - some in very distressed condition!

In the south, the theatre Commissioners were equally

lofty and dismissive. Geoffrey Axworthy (the Sherman), yearning for Mandalay, imported *Zulu* and *Yogi Class.* Taffswazia's potholed capital was then regaled with *Riot Sellers,* a play on the Bristol Native Riots of 1981. Axworthy looked on benignly at indigenous Theatre Wales's first blunders, gloatingly noted, "If things don't work out this time, there won't be another opportunity for at least a decade!" Theatre Wales, now thoroughly confused by good and bad advice, by friends as well as enemies, pressed on with its missed-chances policy of strong Welsh acting in weak West-End hits. The Company's choice of plays lacked local colour but its rows were vividly Welsh.

The Torch's outgoing director, Graham Watkins, was castigated by critic Robert Nesbet in the Western Mail, who called his work "light-weight." Nesbet doubted if Watkins "had ever done much by way of serious theatre." The Torch's new director, Andrew Manly, opened with *The Canterbury Tales.* Nesbet condemned this choice as "bait for school parties" and "an attempt to help justify the theatre's WAC grant." "Nesbet should stop reviewing plays as if they were scripts!" retorted Mr Manly, and had his grant of £114,000 confirmed by the Colony's Arts Commissioners. Clive (Whirling Dervish) Barnes, of Llandovery, finally lost his cool. Cruelly ignoring pleas that the WAC "was too vulnerable to withstand parodies of itself", he flayed the aloof mandarins of the WAC in a satirical pamphlet and a review *Off with the Show!*

The WAC, flailing about for a scapegoat, hit out at Equity and the Musician's Union. In its annual report, it declared that the Union's excessive pay demands would "swamp the individual artist" and "create unemployment in the Arts." Equity Organiser, Chris Ryde, wryly commented, "I would like to think we were as important as alleged."

Welsh Dramatist Network member, Graham Jones, later delivered a talk to Trade Union leaders on The Condition of Theatre in Wales. Strike action was barely avoided.

Throughout 1981-82, regular meetings of writers and dramatists increasingly confirmed the ever-widening gulf between the actual experiences of the dramatists in Welsh theatres and the pious and hollow declarations of the directors on new plays and playwrights.

It was out of this gulf that the Welsh Dramatists Network was born. The Network's first Press Release provoked mixed responses, "Dedwydd Jones has done more damage to the reputation of the Welsh Theatre than anyone I can think of!" (Graham Watkins, The Stage, September 17th, 1981). Watkins also took the opportunity to put those nasty, unseen, Welsh nationalist-terrorist plays in their place: "Dedwydd Jones's plays are pervaded by a chauvinism of the most bizarre and nauseous kind. Chauvinism that would make the National Front pale into reasonableness."

Roger Tomlinson, Administrator of the Mold Theatre, found the dramatists' proposals and recommendations "misleading... inaccurate... remote." The allegiance of this writer to "the idea of a Welsh National theatre" was called "blind" and "splenetic."

**How to Get Rid of the WAC**

The WON at its inaugural meetings, came to two main conclusions: the last place to send Welsh plays were Welsh theatres; how to get Welsh plays on in Wales depended largely on how to get rid of the WAC. Well then - how?

On March 1st, 1981 I wrote to the Prime Minister appealing for a reform of the Welsh Arts Council, "Is it not incredible, Prime Minister, that when your name and mine adorn our tombstones, the present officials of the WAC will still be there, nodding over their waste-paper baskets." And, "Have our Arts officials then become a Society of Embalmers, imbued with infallible notions of their own immortality?" To which Mrs Thatcher graciously responded, "The Prime Minister has asked me to thank you for your recent letter and its enclosure." (The "enclosure" was the first edition of *The Black Book on the Welsh Theatre.* Thereafter, I was able to have the matter raised in the House of Commons: "Unstarred. No. 91. Question to the Prime Minister, tabled 10th April, 1981. Mr Dafydd Wigley to ask the Prime Minister what representations she had recently received from playwright Dedwydd Jones about the structure of the Arts Council in Wales and what reply she has sent him?" This was answered by the Prime Minister on Monday April 13th, 1981: "I received a letter from Mr Jones on 13th March enclosing a letter to my Rt Hon and Learned Friend, the Chancellor of the Exchequer, about the Arts Council in Wales. His letter to me was acknowledged on my behalf on 23rd March." I then immediately circulated an appeal for reform to all interested parties. The replies were prompt, and, mostly, gratifying. Ednyfed Hudson Davies MP (SOP): "I have noted your comments and am in regular discussion with my colleagues on this subject. Again, let me thank you for your concern for the Arts and for making your views public." Keith Best MP (Con), "I am concerned, like you, because it (the WAC) administers public funds and I shall certainly look carefully into the way it exercises its duties." Leo Abse MP (Lab), "Thank you for your letter... "followed by a request for my *Black Book on the Welsh Theatre* so that Mr Foot could "be aware of the views" I "was expressing." From the Court of Pontius Pilate (the Welsh Office) and its Old Guard of Perpetual Hand-Washers, "It has been policy... not to intervene in the decisions of the WAC as regards the direction of its support." Signed, A W G Davies. From Mr Paul Channon, Minister for the Arts, "It is a well established principle that Ministers for the Arts do not intervene in the day to day affairs of the Arts Council."

A constructive proposal came from Dafydd Ellis Thomas MP (Plaid Cymru), member of the Parliamentary Sciences and Arts Committee, "An alternative model (i.e. to the WAC) would be making specific grants to Regional Arts Associations and/or to Local Authorities, and leaving specific decisions on which projects to grant aid to, to be taken locally." From Mr Michael Foot MP (Labour), "It has always been stressed that the Arts Council should have a certain amount of independence." A courteous and helpful reply came from Sir Roy Shaw, Director General of the Arts Council of Great Britain, "I think that the points you raise might be of interest to the House of Commons' Education Science and Arts Committee which is inquiring into the private funding of the Arts in the UK. I am enclosing a Press Note which invites submission of evidence." The Press Note stated, "The Enquiry will cover all aspects of the Arts, visual and performing, and the committee will take written evidence both in the U.K. and abroad. Any organisation or individual wishing to submit evidence should send their submissions to: KW Keeble, Clerk of the Committee, House of Commons." Members of the Welsh Dramatists Network duly submitted such evidence. The Welsh Select Committee was also helpful. From Dr. CRM Ward, Clerk to the Select Parliamentary on Welsh Affairs, "I shall ensure that your proposal (i.e. the reform of the Welsh Arts Council) is put to the Committee when it next considers subjects for enquiry."

Certain of my earlier appeals had received equally gracious notice. From Buckingham Palace: "The Duke of Edinburgh has asked me to thank you for your letter of 11 th November and for sending him a copy of your play *Owen Glyndwr.* His Royal Highness hopes that one day you will see the play performed in the Sherman Theatre." Signed, Commander W B Willett OBE MVO DSC RN. Again, from Buckingham Palace, "Thank you for your letter of 8th November enclosing a copy of your play *Owen Glyndwr.* I am sure the Prince of Wales will accept this with great pleasure and would wish me to send you his sincere thanks for your kind thoughts." Signed, E. Smith MVO, Secretary to the Prince of Wales.

Reactions from fellow dramatists were equally courteous, "I hope to see you in Cardiff and will be able to talk and see what we can do to get your plays on."

(Eugene Ionesco); "Solidarity and exchange of information are so important at this time. All best wishes." (John Arden); "Very best with your work." (John Osborne); "I can only wish you the best of luck." (Harold Pinter). Getting a Welsh play on in Wales in 1981-82 proved, then, as painful and peculiar as ever, but the courtesy, encouragement and sympathy that was freely extended from the highest quarters, certainly heartened and hastened the dramatists in their continuing struggle for the establishment, one day, of a truly Welsh National Theatre.

# Notes in Celebration of St David's Day

March 1,1983

On this unquiet March 1st, singular events continue to haunt Welsh drama. The Play for Wales Competition, for example, unearthed over 150 new Welsh plays --all unplayable. Theatre Wales put on *The Dresser* by South African, R Harwood, but Hywel Bennet, in the lead, walked out. Geoffrey Axworthy (The Sherman, Cardiff) produced Brien Friel's *Translations,* on the grounds that "we wanted to do a play that was relevant to Wales, that's why we're doing a play about Ireland." Director Andrew Manly (The Torch, Milford) put on a four-letter word version of *The Canterbury Tales* by Geoff Chaucer (the founder of the English-Language Society). In spite of the Anglo-Saxonisms, Dyfed loved it. Cardiff dramatist, Carl Tighe, received £3,750 "to write about Gunther Grass's links with Gdansk." Why that last **fifty** pounds? Welshpersoness Kathleen Smith, lacking a native stage, hired the theatre at New End, London, to present her own play --and why not? London stages are the best in Wales!

Roger Tomlinson, out of Mold, by Aberytwyth Arts Centre, was appointed new Drama Director at the Welsh Arts Council. Surveying the familiar, funny old scene, he observed, rather mysteriously, "Ad hoc grants are a dilemma!" --Latin and French with a bit of English thrown in - the WAC status quo in full cliché again!

So, on this unsettled St David's Day, the weird Welsh Theatre cauldron is bubbling away nicely. 0, may this heady, uncanny brew still be sung at a year's turning!

# Review of the Theatre in Wales
## 1983-1985

The temper of Welsh Drama in 1983 and 1984 was uncharacteristically mild. *Moving Being,* for example, "dissociated itself" from performing at the Welsh Tourist Board's "insensitive" Festival of Welsh Castles, pointing out, reasonably enough, that there **were** no Welsh-built castles. This minor nationalist huff caused little furore. The Human Cartoon Theatre Company's *Finger in the Dyke* --"a shock-horror death play about a Lesbian prostitute and a bondage obsessed cop", did, however, arouse a certain Councillor Lewis of Swansea –but only momentarily. Unhappily, Howard Brenton's *The Romans in Britain* pushed him right over the edge. The Councillor had the play banned on the grounds that the imaginary male rape scenes "contributed to sexual assaults in the country." But, for all the outrage, no lasting damage was done.

### A Year of Few Complaints

As noted in a caption to a picture in The Stage, "the exterior" of Cardiff's Sherman Theatre "became ten years old." Local bigwigs celebrated inside with low-profile plays which upset no one. Jane Phillips of the Caricature Theatre saw her grant cut by fifty, then by a hundred percent. She claimed "personal victimization," but --fair-play --the Welsh Arts Council had warned of "maimings by the bureaucratic hatchet." So Miss Phillips's ire went rightly unremarked. The Western Mail summed up such situations explicitly, "Recipients of WAC money have never been entitled to an annuity for life."

The Barnes Management of Llandovery went as far as to publicly wish they "could join the WAC family" and "become legitimized" - a fanciful desire really and outside the WAC's more weighty brief.

Terence James in The Stage (August,1983) even reported "a boost" for Welsh drama. Nine theatres, regardless of size, received vastly increased grants, some "to encourage work with new writers." The WAC's Direct9r, Mr. Aneurin Morgan -Thomas, amiably explained that this "reflected growing confidence in the Companies' ability to present good performances." Cardiff's Chapter Arts Centre accepted its annual £290,000 with customary good grace.

### Happy Writers

1983 was, in short, a year of few complaints. As for playwrights, rancour was almost absent. *The Virgin and the Bull* by Budapest dramatist George Mikes went on at Hungary's Mold Theatre, North Wales. Later, "a follow-up" to *The Mousetrap* was performed - *Swedish* by Lars Lorens. Director Roman's *Faust* unaccountably played to only 30.7 per cent capacity but then Roman candidly confessed that Goethe had been "a foolhardy choice." *Cinderella* soon put the books right and solid doses of Shakespeare, Ayckbourne and Stoppard rapidly dispelled all uncertainties.

In Cardiff, a few short native plays even took the stage. *End of the Bay* and *Canned Goods* by eloquent Dick Edwards, and Sion Eirian's satiric *Crash Course* did much to justify Wales's £1,624,300 drama budget. A new arson play *House to House* showed, too, there was a lighter side to this regional –and quite unnecessary --problem. In the Far West, dramatist Denise Deegan (Torch Theatre, Milford) "spent a long time talking to locals" for her native play *The Harvesters' Feast.* The Director of Theatre Wales, Alan Vaughan-Williams, "the colossus of the short-stemmed pipe," personally directed his fine new work *Matchplay,* which, while winning no accolades, provoked widespread comment.

The newly-formed Welsh Theatre Writers Union, in its first major report, did gently point out one or two minor faults. Made in Wales, for example, had somehow overlooked payments to dramatists, but the number (and the amounts) were very, very small. The Torch Theatre was threatened with legal action for scripts mislaid for two years or more, but this proved to be an exception, as in the past. Playwright Carl Tighe pointed out, "In Wales most companies still do not use a contract with writers." This was duly noted by managements, no doubt for long-term correction. The Union Report, in playful mood, mentioned the nickname of one Welsh theatre --the Black Hole --due, apparently, to irreversible ingestions of scripts.

## We Don't Want to Lose Our Shirts

The Sherman's Geoffrey Axworthy was again quoted on new plays, "We don't want to lose our shirts." New work was fit only "for sort of low-budget try-outs" in the Sherman's post-graduate Arena Theatre. Of his "Critics Circle" he went on: "Writers have enough outlets. Critics have none at all."

The watchword, then, for Welsh Theatre writers during 1983-1984, was "business as usual."


## Plunge into Chaos

In March of 1984, the Director of the WAC went into early retirement. "I have been too long in the job" he told the Press "seventeen years is too long for Art... ingenuity becomes blunted... one's skills may not be a match for the problem." Sir Hywel Evans, Chairman of the WAC, welcomed a Mr. Tom Owen as Mr. Thomas's replacement but Mr. Owen was given a fiveyear contract only, with options for renewal. Mr. Roger Tomlinson, the recently appointed Drama Director (formerly Administrator at the Mold theatre) was given a similar contract. 81 Would the new team "boost" Welsh drama afresh? A slight cautionary note was already detectable. Mr. Roy Bohana, the WAC's Deputy Director, stated, "We will have to be more selective in the way we distribute our funds." But by early summer that nasty old "bureaucratic hatchet" seemed well and truly buried. However, in June of 1984, just before the hols, the scene, as well as the language "plunged into chaos." The WAC was "slammed" as "centralist, reactionary, tyrannous, conspiratorial, dictatorial, despotic, derelict, misleading, interventionist and unilateralist!" News comments were "devastating": "Question marks hung over traditional hot potatoes... "; "Fair and open manners" were lost "in imbecilities of the highest order... "; "Backbones of seasons" were "going to the wall... "; "Livelihoods at stake" were "tossed about behind closed doors... "; "Thin spreadings of the butter" were "smothered in catalogues of non-consultation... "; "Accountability" posed "grave threats" to "non democratic quangos... "; "Naive exercises in arithmetic" abounded... ; "Successful structures" were "killed by certainties of tone."

All this "smacked of not sharing." The WAC was "beseiged" with "hints of mass resignations." There could be no doubt.Major embarassments were abroad! Welsh drama was busting out all over!

The WAC replied with its usual barrage of cotton-wool retractions: "Adoptions of priorities.concentrations of effort... first drafts... strategic reviews... half-way stages... essential functions... new initiatives and shifting commitments."

Artistic Director People, Spokespersons of Theatres, Chiefs of Executives, Union Officer Folk, all added to the chorus. Welsh Equity waded in, as did the Welsh Association for the Performing Arts, the Regional Arts Associations --the titles are still coming in! Theatre Workers demonstrated. WAC officials were forced to use side-doors. Saddest of all, the WAC's own drama committee expressed dissent. The Night of the Long Knives was too blatant even for them. The new Director, however, kept his cool and observed, "What Committees recommend is their dreams" and went on to justify the ways of the WAC to the Select Parliamentary Committee on Welsh Affairs. This body is now sifting remarkable evidence of Welsh Thatcherite viciousness, obduracy and sycophancy.

### Priorities into Practice

What caused the unholy mess this time? The answer is "The Glory of the Garden", the Arts Council of Great Britain's document for Arts cuts and public and private sponsorship. The WAC called its policy-clone "Priorities into Practice." These "priorities" *involved* "putting drama out to tender... on a franchise basis... ". "Suppliants" were "to make bids for three-year contracts." "Cluster managements" and "joint responsibilities" were mooted - and rapidly repudiated by alarmed Artistic Director People. "Miscellaneous sources" were to be "pruned." Chapter Arts Centre, for example, was to somehow cough up a neat, unneeded £17,000. These "priorities" were at once put "into practice."

### Hatchet Work

Theatre Wales became instantly defunct. (The fringe theatres will undoubtedly be picked off one by one, at the WAC's leisure). The WAC after its first announcements, abruptly invited Local Authorities to *cover* the amounts of the cuts. There were prompt refusals. Moving Being came to a rest. "If we don't fund, we'll be to blame," lamented a Cardiff Councillor, "the WAC will wriggle out of it." "This is not the end" proclaimed a Sherman Spokesperson "the Sherman has made a significant contribution to the education of the country." The WAC, in return, promised "a thorough *review* of the Sherman's finances."

The WAC's all-round hatchet work aimed at saving a nifty £527,000. For what purpose? Why --to spend it all over again! This time on two new "large-scale" super-elite, prestigious Repertory Theatres, one for North Wales, and one for the south, in Cardiff. A pressing "priority" for these new theatres was "finding personnel of the right calibre." And who to find them?

The WAC, naturally. On the Orwellian principle that "some people are more equal than others" the WAC, on March 24, 1984, confirmed three key WAC officers in their jobs "until retirement", that is, for life. They were the Finance Director, the Literature Director and the Deputy Director. Two of these have already served the mandatory mind-numbing seventeen years, so in view of their present ages, all three can be expected to be there 'till the year 2001. At that time, they will have served the Welsh Arts for a glorious thirty-seven years. One wonders just" what "blunted skills and ingenuities" will usher Welsh Drama into the next century.


### Look after Number One

But behind the facade and the fake, two-faced shock-horror reactions, there is, in truth, no real sense of surprise at all, just as there is no real belief in a WAC "conspiracy." The WAC has always been a monopoly and its "priorities" have always been the same - money, position, power and permanence for its principal members. Indeed, its topmost priority is as widely admired as it is well known, "Look after Number One!"

Thus, as a monopoly, the WAC has performed admirably. As a bureaucratic arts achievement, it is unique in the UK. As a patron of Welsh drama, its putrefying remains have long been interred - mainly by Welsh dramatists.

Out of all this, then, who cares? We, the writers who still serve the Muse and do not manipulate her for gain, we who have given over our lives to her with no great hopes for a living, we who still revere her can do but one thing: set it all down, as before, making it known we are still at our desks, still trying, still recording the truth of drama and of life --though we labour at our craft in a wilderness.

Swansea Grand Theatre, the most elegant theatre in Wales.

# Drama Franchise Fiasco

## 1985

The Welsh Drama Franchise Fiasco of '85 was undoubtedly won. £625,000 went to someone. Two jobs were instantly created (for a production manager and a marketing officer). Splendid! But for how many? And who exactly got the moola? Was it Geoffrey Axworthy's favourite holiday home, the Sherman Theatre? Or University College, Cardiff, with its annual £100,000 stake in "the building"? Or the Sherman's postgrad Arena theatre? Or the Made in Wales Company? And who is now boss? Double Director Geoffrey and "his" main Sherman stage? Or, again, "his" Arena, with its graduate-amateur chieftains? Or Mike James, triple director of the Arena (or is it the Sherman main?) formerly of (or still with?) Made in Wales. Or the WAC's formidable new trouble-shooter (or is it "maker"?), Roger Tomlinson? (There is no doubt that Roger is doing a marvellous job - but just what **is** his job?) And who gets those seven major and two minor (or is it vice versa?) production grants? Is the whole ghastly £625,000 a "divide and rule" tactic?

And if so, who is the ruler and who the ruled? Whatever the answer, there is no doubt that the Sherman has been saved "from nose-diving into educational backwaters" and given "what it has needed for years - a sense of direction" - 625,000 directions, in fact.

Theatre Wales, now slightly defunct, immediately asserted there *was* life after the Franchise. Director Alan (the-Colossus- of-the of the-Short-:Stemmed-Pipe) Vaughan Williams, believed that "his" theatre's

107

existence was still "second to none in Wales." The "Welsh Arts Chiefs" of Clwyd (Mold, North Wales), slammed the Welsh Arts Council's carve up: "Irresponsible!... Wales should be seen as a whole." Mold's new Saxon Supremo, Toby Robertson, waded into his first Welsh theatre brawl and slammed the Sherman's victory as "a financial convenience." Toby's own administrator, Patric Gilchrist, slammed all the slammers, including his boss, and swore Mold was "neither surprised nor disappointed." Mold's former bold administrator, Roger (WAC) Tomlinson, slammed back, "The WAC conducted interviews for the franchise... headed by the Chairman of the WAC!" Gilly Adams, the WAC's former bold administrator (now a bold independent theatre director, with "Salvation" behind her), slammed the former bold administrator at Mold, Roger (WAC) Tomlinson, who had just slammed the current bold administrator at Mold, who had... "In my time there was always growth!" slammed on Gilly, regardless.

One bewildered Theatre Writers Union (TWU) member mused, "The same old shit's appearing on all the other boots, but damned if I know who's wearing the boots!"

Roger (WAC) Tomlinson's fine Franchise Apologia in the Western Mail (December 28th, 1984), is already a classic of sparkling directorese, wherein "honeymoon periods" flirted with "important watersheds"; "major deterrents" rubbed shoulders with "blazes of glory" and "hand to mouth existences"; where "major responsibilities" mixed with "underlying concerns" and "grass roots"; where "thorny problems" and "high profiles" were found "making strides" at "crisis level"; "arguments",too, were "boiled down" to "reassess directions" in "gaps in provision".

One awed TWU dramatist suggested that in future "0" Level English be made obligatory for all WAC "officers". Another playwright wondered if "the present system of appointment to the WAC, where a candidate is nominated by the Arts Council of Great Britain and then approved by the Secretary of State for Wales", was "entirely satisfactory."

The theatre writers then turned their astonished gaze on the Torch, Milford, as the new semi-imported inner-city Director, Les (Boot-in-both-Camps) Miller, announced his first season of plays, *Hay Fever, Elephant Man, A Midsummer Night's Dream* and *Having* a *Ball* (recently seen at Mold). Swansea Grand's playbill boasted, *Babes in the Wood,* a *Mr Cinders* and *Hi-de-Hi!* The casuality roll of contemporary dramatists mounted rapidly. Theatre Powys came up with a *Julius Caesar* which mirrored "the military society of ancient Rome in the context of present day society."

Made in Wales gave us the Russian *Goverment Inspector* with "a strong Welsh 1920's flavour." Cardiff's Laboratory Theatre updated Churchill's funeral "in the context of the demise of Gwyn the Fish."

Wales's Reign of Saints continued its dirty work and Keith Miles's *Lady Chatterly's Lover* was banned in Cardiff "on moral grounds." Anti-Aids kits were handed out at Swansea's Taliesin Theatre after gay Sweatshop's production of *Poppies.* A theatre spokesperson stated that the issue of rubber gloves to the cleaning staff "had been blown up out of all proportion." "Charming" Hungarian Director George Roman of Mold finally hung up his buskins; his "swan song" - *"Witness for the Prosecution"* by Agatha Christie; Roman's last word - "a new energy and different ideas... are important." Toby (First Brawl) Robertson (see above) was thereafter imported by the Welsh worthies of Mold - who have their fingers on the pulse - of London!

The main stages of Wales are again controlled one hundred per cent by outsiders.

In April, Made in Wales launched its "Write On", a programme of new talking set somewhere in the Sherman Complex. Very short plays were spoken on very small stages (or podiums) while the main Sherman stage remained untainted by the scribbling, scrappy Taffies. Lively dissensions followed between "actors, directors, writers and audiences."

Members of the TWU had meanwhile been hard at research and the second "Playwrights' Register" was published (edited by Carl Tighe). The Register pointed out that new plays were possible - in England: "Between 1980 and 1983, Derby, Stoke and Coventry Reps offered a total of 18 new plays between them... In less than three seasons, Birmingham Rep offered 13 new plays." Carl Tighe neatly summed up the fate of new Welsh plays, "In Wales, the annual yield is 100 scripts; this means (given the record) that an unsolicited script will reach the stage once every ten years... the next one should be seen in Wales in the year 1993."

The Register noted that there were some 800 playwrights who wrote for Welsh stages. The Theatre

Writers Union is the first and only organization which gives absolute preference to Welsh dramatists. The TWU now offers the sole hope of solidarity between Welsh writers and their home theatres. All our dramatists are, therefore, urged, firstly, to join the TWU; secondly, to communicate all instances of abuse, incompetency, unprofessionalism and anti-Welsh discrimination they have encountered or might encounter, in theatres in Wales. It is the theatre writers alone who can provide a permanent and true record of the real condition of Welsh theatre. It is they alone who can finally free their own stages. Without Welsh plays there is no Welsh theatre.

# Arts Council under Fire from Playwrights

An "autocratic" Welsh Arts Council has come under heavy fire from a group of angry playwrights who claim that their work isbeing ignored in their home country.

The recently formed Welsh Dramatists Network has called forwide-ranging reforms of the WAC to ensure that more work byEnglish-writing Welsh dramatists is performed in theatres in Wales.And the Network - a loose association of prominent writers which includes Dedwydd Jones, Dannie Abse, Alun Rees and       Clive Paton - is compiling a dossier of the difficulties experienced by its members, to be distributed to newspapers, MP's, Select Parliamentary Committees and the Arts Council of Great Britain. Spokesman for the group, Dedwydd Jones, told The Stage that Welsh dramatists writing in English have been "banging their heads against brick walls" for years, trying to get their work staged in Welsh theatres, and that the time had come when the WAC and theatres must be seen to be making positive efforts to tip the scales in their favour.

Welsh-speaking theatre is relatively well catered for, he said, even though it had suffered financially. Theatres in Wales were relying on established classics such as Brecht and Ayckbourn rather than tapping the home talent.

But Jones laid the blame for the poor showing of English writing Welsh dramatists squarely on the shoulders of the Welsh Arts Council which, he claims, has become "an autocratic body of the Pontius-Pilate type - continually washing its hands of the situation."

"There is no other grant-giving body in Wales, unlike in Scotland or England, and most of the Council's personnel have been there since 1967, so attitudes are difficult to change," he explained.

"When we ask theatres why they don't run seasons of plays by English-writing Welsh dramatists, they say there is no money left. There is nobody but the Council to appeal to and the theatres imitate the Council and its autocratic attitude."

The Network now wants to see the WAC take a lead in reversing the situation, he added, but the only way that this could be achieved is by reforming the body and its policies.

The issue is crucial because many writers have given up producing work for the theatre and are turning increasingly to television.

Many have no difficulty having their work produced in England, Scotland or even America but find it impossible to do the same in their own country.

"We have had terrific sympathy from Westminster and the Arts Council in London... but when we go to the Welsh Office or to the WAC, we are up against a blank wall," said Jones.

A spokesman for the WAC told The Stage that senior members of the WAC were unavailable for comment due to the holiday period.

The Stage, August 6th, 1981

## Discrimination Claim by Welsh Writers

The Parliamentary Committee for Welsh Affairs is to consider investigating the Welsh Arts Council after allegations by leading Welsh writers that their works are seldom performed in the Principality.

According to the writers, they are being made strangers in their own land because of "the ossified and rigid" nature of the Council, which they claim is unwilling to present bold or controversial works.

The writers, led by Dedwydd Jones, the prize-winning playwright, who is supported by Dannie Abse, Gwyn Clark and other eminent playwrights, have formed a Welsh dramatist network to tip the scales in favour of English-language Welsh plays in Welsh theatres.

Their ultimate aim is the establishment of a Welsh National Theatre where indigenous drama can be performed. Mr Jones said: "The Welsh Arts Council prefers to play safe by financing tried and safe classical plays. Its resistance to anything new from Welsh writers is stifling.

"The Council has been here for a long time and I feel the whole set-up must be transformed if theatre in Wales is to become alive and exciting. What makes theatre in Wales so vulnerable is that the Council is the only grant-funding body in the land. This monopoly position means that its influence is all pervasive."

Mr Jones continued: "We hope sufficient evidence of discrimination, ignorance and arrogance on the part of the WAC will accumulate and justify a case for its abolition and replacement with a fairer and more practical body."

He believes that the Welsh establishment is too vulnerable to withstand parodies of itself. That, he thinks, is summed up by George Bernard Shaw, who wrote in 1914 about a proposed Welsh national theatre:

"Everything that is narrow and ignorant and ridiculous and dishonest in Wales will be castigated ruthlessly by the theatre and the process will not be popular with the narrow, the ignorant, the bigoted and the ridiculous." "Over the border nobody cares enough about Wales to tell her the truth about herself; to rub into her conscience the glaring faults of her striking qualities.

Shaw added: "If Wales thinks that a National Theatre will be a place where her praises will be sounded continually, where the male villain will be an Englishman of the Church of England and the female villain a French spy or a bishop's wife, whilst the hero (being a Welshman) will be insufferably noble and the heroine (being a Welshwoman) too good for this earth, Wales will be disappointed.

"Just as the preachers of Wales spend much of their time in telling the Welsh that they are going to hell, so the Welsh writers of comedy will have to console a good many of them by demonstrating that they are not worth wasting good coal on." It is this kind of fear which, Mr Jones says, has prevented the growth of a bold, healthy and critical theatrical tradition in the Principality. No spokesman from the Welsh Arts Council was available for comment..

The Times, August 17th, 1981

**The Welsh Dramatists' Network**

**Second Press Release**

To prevent further wastages of public funds, the Welsh Dramatists Network (WDN) calls at once for a stop to all Welsh Arts Council Theatre grants until the Parliamentary Committee investigating the Arts has sifted its evidence and issued its findings. The WDN condemns utterly the continuing ruinous absence of any overall plan or policy in theatre grants, especially as they affect Welsh playwrights.

The WDN also condemns the unbridled prejudice displayed by the Welsh Arts Council and the main theatres of Wales, against Welsh dramatists. At best, the dramatists continue to be regarded as embittered, unwashed bohemians to be avoided at all costs, or, at worst, irrelevant nuisances to be ignored or insulted as the occasion arises. The pathetic financial scraps tossed both to the playwrights and to small companies trying to present new work, can only intended to hold up indigenous talent to contempt and ridicule.

From among many examples, the WDN further condemns the following recent bureaucratic outrages:

## 1. The System of Awarding Theatre Grants

The Welsh Arts Council's grants to Theatre Wales are typical of all grants made to new companies. Each grant is made on an ad-hoc one-off basis. Every further grant is made dependant on the "success" of the preceding venture. This system, in the absence of a long-term policy, merely tends to provoke rivalries,discord and fragmentation - as, indeed, happened with Theatre Wales. Also, it allows official, arbitrary termination of "unpopular" groups, such as the now defunct Bag and Baggage Company.The WON calls for a system in which the WAC is made publically accountable for its decisions.

## 2. Grants to Outsiders

The WON condemns the Arts Council's incomprehensible grant of £16,000 to the new-image Theatre Wales for a production of Irishman Brien Friel's play *Translations,* and this at a time when the new Welsh group Made in Wales was forced to present Cardiff dramatist Nick Edwards' play "on a shoe-string budget" for one night only.

The WON calls for a total ban on all grants to outsiders as long as one Welsh writer or one Welsh theatre group has to go begging.

## 3. The "Play for Wales" Competition

From the start of this competition, not one major theatre in Wales made any commitment whatsoever to a production of the winning play, nor was one penny set aside by the WAC to support such a production. Ultimately, the winners were fobbed off with a "prize" of five hundred pounds and "rehearsed readings." (JF Thomas's winning play was not presented at all on the grounds that the author "lived in New Zealand.") The WON expresses its disgust at this shoddy and unprofessional treatment.

### 4. The Grant to Swansea Grand Theatre

The grant of £600,000 by the WAC to Swansea Grand Theatre for "improvements over the next five years" proves conclusively that long-term commitments can be made - but, apparently, only to like-minded theatre bureaucrats. No provision whatsoever has been made for the presentation of Welsh work in this Welsh theatre. Presumably, the WAC merely intends to swell its list of pseudo-swank white elephant theatres for the sole benefit of its fellow travellers..

### 5. The Appointment of Artistic Directors

The WON deplores the continuing appointment of outsiders to the few theatre jobs available in Wales. Such theatres rapidly become places where non-Welsh material is presented. The WON demands that in future the appointment of writers, actors and technicians should be of Welsh people only. The WON further declares that all future grants to theatres should be made dependant on giving employment primarily to Welsh theatre artists.

## 6. The Treatment of Scripts

The WON *reserves* its most profound expression of disgust for the treatment accorded to scripts submitted to theatres in Wales. Such treatment *varies* from outright loss, unacknowledged retention of scripts for interminable periods, impolite disclaimers of the receipt of posted scripts, to final, one-line, coffee-stained, crumpled rejections. Such treatment, all experienced by WON members, provides the ultimate proof of the contempt in which the indigenous dramatist is held, in his *native* Wales.

### Conclusion

Sir Hywel Evans, the new Chairman of the WAC, has declared that he wants "to bring some Real 'vim' into the whole theatre scene." The WON would like to point out that it is not 'vim' that is needed - the writers have always provided plenty of that - but a plan or policy and a long-term commitment. The Welsh Arts Council is as uncommited now as it has been during the whole of its miserable fifteen-year monopoly. The WON, therefore, calls for a cessation to all theatre grants until the Parliamentary Committee on the Arts has published its findings.

Lastly, the WON wishes to remind all Welsh writers of the words of the official Parliamentary Press Release, "Any organisation or individual wishing to submit evidence (on the Arts in Wales) should send their submissions to the Clerk of the Committee of Education, Science and the Arts, House of Commons, London SW1."

We urge all Welsh writers to submit evidence now!

June 14th, 1982

## Freeze **on WAC Grants**

All theatre grants from the Welsh Arts Council should be frozen until the Parliamentary Committee currently investigating the state of the arts in the principality publishes its findings.

The demand has come from the Welsh Dramatists Network in a strong statement condemning the WAC's handling of theatre funding. "Grants should be frozen to *prevent* further wastages of public money," the group says.

*Over* the past few years, the WAC has been under attack from many groups in Wales. Its decision to axe £60,000 grant to the Welsh magazine *Arcade* finally precipitated a Parliamentary enquiry into the funding of the body's affairs. The committee has been gathering *evidence* from many arts groups in Wales *over* the past few months and isexpected to announce its findings soon.

The Welsh Dramatists Network's complaints hinge upon what it calls the "continuing ruinous absence of an *overall* plan or policy in theatre grants, especially as they affect playwrights." "The Welsh Arts Council's grants to Theatre Wales are typical of all grants to new companies. Each grant is made on an ad hoc, one-off basis. Each further grant is made dependent on the success of the preceding venture. "

The group also claims there is an "unbridled prejudice" displayed by the WAC and the main theatres of Wales against Welsh dramatists. "The pathetic financial scraps tossed to 101 playwrights and small scale companies trying to present new work can only be intended to hold up indigenous talent to contempt and ridicule."

Attempts have been made to stimulate interest in and acceptance of Welsh dramatists by the recent "Play for Wales" competition, but the WON claims that "not one major theatre in Wales made any commitment whatsoever to a production of the winning play nor was one penny set aside to support such a production."

Director of the Welsh Arts Council, Aneurin Thomas, said that he had not received the statement from the WON and if the group "had had the courtesy to send me a copy I would have brought it to the attention of officers at the Council.

"It would therefore be unwise to make detailed comments on the statements but if what I have heard about it is correct, I would say that their accusations are unfounded.

It would be quite improper to suspend our normal activities pending the Parliamentary report which I believe is largely irrelevant to the points made in the WDN's statement," he said.

The Stage, July 1st, 1982

Letters to the Press

**(in chronological Order)**


**Playwrights**

SIR, - As a dramatist, the recent correspondence in The Stage has been of great interest.

The laments on the fate of new plays have been many. However, I would point out that a dramatist does not submit his work to "establishments" but to individual "Artistic Directors."

Way back in the good old days of 1967, submission to Artistic Directors was a weird enough experience. In 1974 an even weirder, indeed, Kafkaesque, experience awaits the dramatist.

To enter a theatre now is to enter the unreal twilight world of dramaturges, literary advisers, consultants and experts, assistant directors, visiting directors, trainee directors, juvenile directors, adapters, devisers, translators, arrangers, readers, researchers, composers, french-horn players, clowns, acrobats, dogs and frequently, groups of instant dramatists uttering spontaneous dialogue of deathless beauty. If one mentions the words "my play," one is treated to streams of aesthetic gibberish. At this point, grab the play and run.

In the spring of 1973, I carried out an experiment. I sent out forty copies of a new play, all to Artistic Directors. To this day, I have received back exactly three. As a dramatist, therefore, in 1974, I have given up sending plays to theatres.

But still as a dramatist, how do I get my work performed? Apply to the Arts Council? Never. No dramatist in the UK can now apply direct for either a bursary, or for a production grant for one of his plays. A dramatist has to be sponsored by an Artistic Director, a dramaturge, a literary advisor, consultant, etc. But still as a dramatist, how do I get my work performed? The answer is not to do any of the things your correspondents have so far suggested. A dramatist must not "fight" the theatres. He can't, simply because theatres are much better financed against such involvements. What a dramatist must do, is **not** submit his work through the usual channels. The doors of the theatre may be closed but drama is still wide open. A dramatist must personally call on anyone who is connected with the theatre who is not an Artistic Director. He must call on individual actors, individual theatre enthusiasts, and known individual backers. By using this approach, I was able, last year, to produce two of my own plays with actor Jon Finch as both patron and backer. I am now planning a similar event for next June.

It is to be noted that this method represents the traditional English combination of actor-manager-writer, a tradition which includes such names as Shakespeare, Garrick, Sheridan, Henry Irving, Granville- Barker, Lady Gregory, and, at present, Sir Bernard Miles, the last major representative of the great English tradition of actor-manager-writer. I therefore urge dramatists at least to try this method before they use the usual channels.

Lastly, it is neither Artistic Directors, nor managements, actors or dramatists, who are the final arbiters of a play. It is the public and the public alone who are, and they pay cash for the privilege. Ultimately, of course, time really is the final arbiter. However, the danger for the new dramatist today is that he will be long dead before either audience or time make an assessment of his work.

Dedwydd Jones, Creigiau, Nr. Cardiff, Wales

The Stage, January 1 st, 1974


**No Welsh Theatre in Wales**

SIR, - In Peter Davies's recent article on the Celtic Theatre, he reproves the Welsh for "referring to mythology and history to remind themselves who they are."

As far as the theatre (English-speaking) is concerned, this is quite inaccurate. The simple fact is that that in Wales there is no Welsh "theatre." Hence, there is no Welsh theatre mythology or history to refer to in the first place.

The so-called "Welsh" Drama Company in its recent season, gave us a play by a dead Russian, a living Englishman, and a long-departed Anglo-Irish dramatist. This can hardly be called "subservience" to Welsh "mythology."

The "traditions" to which the Welsh Drama Company addresses itself are traditions which would shame the most moribund of English provincial repertory companies. Thus in the theatre we have no "ancestors" to "retard our progress." There is not only no progress - not even a start has been made.

As far as Welsh plays are concerned, I would refer Mr Davies to two plays --the first *Taffy* by Caradoc Evans. This play was first performed in London in 1924 (ironically enough, at the Prince of Wales Theatre) and was a huge success.

*Taffy* helped Caradoc Evans to earn the title of "the most hated man in Wales." Mr Evans earned this title for assaulting the very "traditions and mythologies" which Mr Davies finds such a hindrance. It is precisely because of these attacks that, to this day, *Taffy* has never once been performed in Wales.

Lastly, I have myself written more than thirty plays. Of these, only two have been on specifically Welsh subjects, and of these, one holds up to ridicule certain Welsh "mythologies and traditions." I am, moreover, too old to wait sixty years for a rejection, and English theatres, anyway, really are interested in Welsh plays, especially if they happen to praise Welsh "mythologies."

Until a Welsh theatre "mythology" is born, Welsh dramatists, actors and audiences cannot even paddle in "traditions" let alone "drown in them."

Dedwydd Jones, Creigiau, Nr Cardiff, Wales

The Western Mail, March 13th, 1974

**Writers, Swap your Nationality...**

SIR, - So writer Fred Durrenmatt now leaves Wales richer by £1,000 sterling, a much needed currency in his native Switzerland no doubt. Meanwhile, Welsh writers who live outside Wales, even as far afield as England, are still automatically barred from Welsh Arts Council support. But Welsh writers should draw the logical conclusion from this grand international hand-out. They should all immediately go and live abroad, as I have recently done. I know now, that as a Welsh writer, all I have left to do to qualify for Welsh Arts Council support, is to apply for Swiss citizenship.

So Welsh writers out of Wales, don't despair, just swap nationalities -and you're home.

Dedwydd Jones, Lausanne, Switzerland

The Western Mail, February 19th, 1976

**Despair over Welsh Theatre**

SIR, - With seasons of new plays now being announced for the main theatres of Wales, one increasingly despairs of ever seeing any programme which even faintly reflects Welsh needs and interests. Again we have *Macbeth,* or is it *Lear?* Or *The School for Scandal,* or is it *St. Joan* ? --all the plays which have already been seen a thousand times on film and TV and in schools and universities.

In 1916, GB Shaw wrote, "If Manchester, Dublin and Glasgow produced an indigenous drama almost instantly upon the establishment of a theatre, what might Wales not do with its wealth of imagination and adventurousness?" We now have four major theatres in Wales, more on the way, but with nothing planned of permanent, regional interest to put into them. And not only are these large theatres artistically bankrupt, they are financially bankrupt, too. Mold, for example, has to pay over £100,000 per annum in loan charges alone. Are these massive losses (or "subsidies" as they are now called) really necessary? Martin Williams, of the Cardiff New Theatre, has proved that plays **can** pay. Our smaller native groups, Theatr Yr Ymylon and Pryderi and his Pigs, and the smaller theatres at Berwyn and Canton, Cardiff, also demonstrate that there is an alternative.

If the Shavian idea of an indigenous drama can be said to exist at all in Wales, it can exist only in the above-mentioned smaller groups, and theatres, and for these reasons: These groups are primarily the result of individual imagination and enterprise. They primarily reflect local interests. They primarily give jobs to Welshmen and Welsh women. They do not possess huge theatres to bankrupt their plays. They do not imitate bankrupt, central models simply because they are English. They are prepared to cultivate what they have, and not to import what they cannot grow.

Until one such native, smaller group is put on an equal footing in terms of power, permanence and money with the major theatres, and until Wales and her Welshmen can develop their own theatres, in their own way, for their own people, in equality first, then Wales simply will never ever have her own indigenous drama at all.

Dedwydd Jones, Lausanne, Switzerland

The Western Mail, February 14th, 1977


**Squabbling English**

SIR, - Geoffrey Axworthy, Michael Geliot, Bill Dutton, Roger Tomlinson - what a refreshing change to see Englishmen squabbling among themselves. Meanwhile, what about a truly Welsh National Theatre?

Dedwydd Jones, Lausanne, Switzerland

The Western Mail, May 1 st, 1977

**This Pauper's Charter**

SIR, - I note that the Welsh Arts Council still persists in presenting its hopeless pauper's charter (Invitation to Writers for Bursaries, 1978-79). To qualify for the WAC's twelve-month dole, a writer must, apparently, first forswear a job, salary, prospects and future. If he lives over the border, he must also forswear home and friends to live in Wales, and he must do this twelve months before he can qualify for the merry-making – twelve months of unemployment which might well be spent in looking for employment.

But if the writer writes to write, and not to publish, he's out anyway, for to the WAC, a writer must first be published before he can write. But even if he has been published, a poet, for example, cannot apply for paid leave to write a play, for a bursary poet is a poet only when he has a bursary. If, therefore, a writer prefers his job, his hearth, his writing and his poetry, to this invited twelve-month dole, he has no hope in WAC Wales. I suggest the following alternative ad:

"Applications for bursaries are invited by the WAC from all Welsh writers, of all ages, resident in Wales, or anywhere else. The applicants do not need to have had anything published before. All applicants must keep their jobs, for jobs are scarce. A writer can write in any medium he pleases, and in Welsh or in English. This year the WAC has given over the decision on 1978 bursaries to Yr Academi Gymraeg, Welsh-and English-speaking sections. All manuscripts will be read by its members and a democratic secret ballot will decide who should be awarded the bursaries. The WAC emphasizes that all writers must produce a finished work at the end of the bursary year, otherwise the writer is disqualified from any further bursaries for life."

Until some such alternative "invitation" is presented, the WAC's pauper's charter will continue to be as irrelevant to Welsh writers and writing anywhere, as it is in 1978-79.

Dedwydd Jones, Lausanne, Switzerland

The Western Mail, February 21 st, 1978


**How Open is this Forum?**

SIR, - If the Welsh Arts Council's "Open Forum" at Aberystwyth later this month is an example of the new "democratisation" of the Council, it could hardly be less auspicious. It is obviously no coincidence that the Forum is to be held on the outskirts of a town deep in mid-Wales far from the main centres of population, well off the main bus and train routes, at the end of the holiday, during school term, in library premises of limited seating capacity.

*Moreover,* entry to this grand public debate is to be by ticket. Applications must be made out to --yes! --the Welsh Arts Council itself. The whole gambit thus arouses the *very* distrust it is supposed to dispel. Such "new democratisations" remind me of the old ones - an ill omen indeed.

Dedwydd Jones, Lausanne, Switzerland

The Western Mail, September 21 st, 1978

SIR, - A brief word in reply to Messrs "Misleading and Inaccurate." My information ref the Torch and Mold Theatres comes from the Torch and Mold Theatres. Surely Mr Tomlinson remembers sending me the details from his own office? I have it all on file.

And surely Mr Watkins, too, remembers my own fact-finding visit to his theatre? My sources are public and available to all press releases, news stories, reviews, official reports, etc. I also still *have* copious notes from the period 1969-75 when I worked in the theatre in Wales. Two of these years were spent as a Fellow in Drama at the Sherman Theatre, a period rich in human experience --which is now being written up.

My Cardiff home is 68 Miskin Street, two hundred yards from the front entrance of the Sherman Theatre. I shall be there in one week, and if Mr Tomlinson or Mr Watkins or anyone else cares to drop in, they would be most welcome. They might even then begin to answer the points raised in my articles, for their written replies have provided absolutely no answers at all.

Dedwydd Jones, Lausanne, Switzerland

The Stage, March 29th,1979

**Nothing for the Arrogant Scribes**

SIR, - So the Welsh Arts Council has decided to drop, if only for a year, its baleful and pernicious bursaries system. But only for writers - due no doubt to their nasty remarks and silly criticisms.

130

Why this comic cut at all? Because of a "cash shortage"! Out of three million in subsidies, not tuppence for those arrogant scribes. Teach that lot a lesson! Show them who's boss!

But what I'd really like to know is just how much the Director of Literature is cutting his benefits by? One-hundred per cent?

Dedwydd Jones, Lausanne, Switzerland

The Western Mail, April 11th, 1979


### We Are the Frankensteins

SIR, - So the Llandovery Theatre is "too exclusive"? So what? Every other major theatre in Wales is. The theatre directors of Mold, Aberystwyth, Swansea, Milford, etc, excercise an absolute authority. There is no court of appeal. The Welsh Arts Council, too, follows the same pattern. Its officers are in for life. Again, no court of appeal.

So why belly-ache? After all, it is us, the Welsh, who created these monsters. The "exclusive", Llandovery Theatre is innocent!

It is us who are guilty. We are the Frankensteins.

Dedwydd Jones, Cardiff, Wales

The Western Mail, September 4th, 1979


### Simple Cure

SIR, - To those who are neither Welsh nor professional theatre people, your paper's persistent healthy airing of the crisis in Welsh professional theatre is worrying.

Such "policy" as expressed by the director of Wales' "national showcase" is a reductio ad absurdum when it advocates festivals of mime. A Theatre of Silence? Small wonder troupes visiting the Sherman have never heard of Wales!

Everyone must realize by now that the future of the professional theatre in Wales - as in the rest of Britain - is not just murder by VAT. The theatrical white elephants of Wales must find their Welsh actors and Welsh dramatists as called for by M. Geliot, Dedwydd Jones and all the rest of the Welsh professionals. Otherwise whence the set-books of the future? There is no longer an abstract, aesthetic argument It concerns only the history, culture and language of Wales but also millions of pounds of taxpayers' money. The cure is simple and quick. The disease will prove lingering, painful and fatal.

John Nicholson, Bedford, England

The Stage, April 30th, 1980


### Checking the Facts

SIR, - Andrew Manly, of Milford's Torch, as a new boy, should really check his facts. He states in his letter (The Stage, August 20th) that "his" triple bill is "all Welsh." Wyckham and Furnival are hardly Welsh names, though Jenkins, the name of the third dramatist,is. The three dramatists in the triple bill, are, in fact, Irish, English and Welsh.

As to the Torch's non-existent "consistent" support of Welsh dramatists, I would refer him to my articles in The Stage over the years, particularly the 9th March, 1978 article. The Torch's percentage of "Welsh" work is a "consistent" one per cent.

The Torch is, of course, one of the Welsh Arts Council's newly dependent poor relations, but this is no excuse for Manly's blind support for a body which suffers from galloping myopia. The WAC dispenses over a million pounds per annum on drama. This adds up to a lot of power.

The Welsh mediocrities who squander these funds and who persist in supporting ill-informed outsiders are as culpable as the English mediocrities themselves, whose ignorance only serves to perpetuate the WAC's fourteen-year monopoly.

As for "opening a dialogue", this is what all members of the Welsh Dramatists Network have been trying to do for the last fifteen years. After Manly has himself tried "opening a dialogue" for that length of time, he might understand, if he is still in Wales, just why the members of the Network regard his statements as just another example of slavish, futile and alien gobbledygook.

Dedwydd Jones, Lausanne, Switzerland

The Stage, September 3rd, 1981

**Damaging Welsh Theatre?**

SIR, - Dedwydd Jones' letter in The Stage (September 3rd) is yet another example of the cockeyed misinformation from this expatriate Welshman who is the most ill-informed outsider of them all.

There is surely something dubious about a writer referring a readership to previous articles in The Stage as arbitration of truth when most of the articles he refers to were written by him and thoroughly informed in the first place.

Whilst I ran the Torch for four years, Oedwydd Jones was allowed to continually pour his invective on practicing artists and WAC alike, through the medium of your pages. Most of what he said during that time was spurious: glaring factual errors went unchecked, errors which he made because he does not live in Wales and is completely out of touch with the real theatrical scene there. He has done more damage to the reputation and proper development of the theatre in Wales than anyone I can think of. Why does he do this?

Maybe he is frustrated because his plays tend not to be produced in Wales. He wrote a treatise for the salvation of the Welsh theatre, or some such pretentious title, some few years ago, and sent it to various theatre practitioners. They treated it with the contempt it deserved because an integral part of it seemed to be the necessity of producing as many Dedwydd Jones plays as possible.

I have, and had, in Milford a genuine desire to produce new works (hence the writer's workshops etc, I set up in Milford). I found it impossible to produce a Oedwydd Jones play because they are often pervaded by a chauvinism of the most bizarre and nauseous kind. Chauvinism which would make the National Front pale into reasonableness.

As is clear in his letter, Dedwydd Jones's definition of what is acceptably Welsh is so narrow it becomes laughable. To start with, people laughed at Nazis measuring noses to decide on the Jewishness of prisoners. The laughing stopped. No one laughs at apartheid's league table of acceptability based on colour. I used to laugh at Dedwydd but now I can look with more objectivity from outside the principality.

I find his fact-twisting and insistent debasement of those genuinely trying to develop a broadly-based Welsh theatre repugnant and sinister.

Graham Watkins, The Phoenix Theatre, Leicester

The Stage, September 17th, 1981


**Desolate**

SIR, - I was desolate to read (The Stage, September 17th) that Graham Watkins's exile in steamy Taffswazia had so unhinged him. If he had ever left the Colonial Club he ran (The Torch), he might have discovered that the "nauseous" natives do, in fact, possess a civilization of their very own --a civilization, moreover, that has little to do with Jewish noses, South African burghers, the National Front, or even with the "disgusteds of Cheltenham"

(or is it Leicester now?).

As to "facts" about the Torch Club, I have only ever quoted those given out in signed and dated letters by Brigadier Watkins or by his aides de camp. Obviously it's not only the native gadflies that have so disoriented the fella, but those confounded harps as well, eh what, Carruthers?

Dedwydd Jones, Lausanne, Switzerland

The Stage, October 1 st, 1981


**Such a Parody**

Dear Dedwydd, - Or should it be Dear Graham? At first I couldn't believe it. The letter in The Stage claiming to come from Graham Watkins is such a parody that I thought that you must have written it! I thought - surely Watkins himself daren't put out such a public statement? Then the awful truth sank in - yes, it is genuine. Not only did Watkins send this abusive letter for publication but he really did offer it as his alternative policy for "a broadly based Welsh theatre."

It's so horrific, it's ridiculous. But this man was in power (four years he controlled a theatre in Wales!) so he was able to put his policy into practice. He even boasts of it. Like others, I had believed your Stage articles were exaggerated for comic effect. It couldn't really be so awful, otherwise... Watkins destroys this hope. He has spelled it out so badly that nobody can ever hide from the truth again. He has given a public statement of the policy which rules the theatres in Wales. For this, everyone mustbe grateful. Never before has the policy been available. Watkins proves there **is** a policy; not an ad hoc muddle of greed and vanity, as you suggested.

This policy makes me ashamed --as an Englishman and as a theatre-lover. It shames me as an Englishman

136

because it is so arrogantly imperialistic. I am always amazed that the English can deny they are fiercely nationalistic when they insist that their way of life is the only proper one. I am sure I am far from alone in having assumed such attitudes were dead and buried. That is my excuse for not believing it was as bad as you painted. If you were right then these people were going to set the clock back over a century. How awful to find you weren't exaggerating. You warned us and we didn't listen and now **we** are paying the price. These dinosaurs have returned from their hide-outs in the Welsh caves to stamp all over **our** country. "There is no alternative" rules us, too.

I am sure none of these points needs making to you. It is people like Watkins who thrive on keeping us apart. They will build their cloud-cuckoo kingdoms in both our countries and erase both our cultures. As Jan Morris said, your articles have vividly described both these cultures and how they differ. Now along comes Watkins to prove how right you were. On the one side is your simple call for a native culture to express itself in its own land. On the other side is Watkins boasting of his determination to prevent this happening. How these cultures differs is clear from examining their different approaches.

Your Plan offered two new ideas - one, a long-term aim (the immediate establishment of an indigenous Welsh drama) and, two - how to achieve this aim (a consistent, public policy). That was the Welsh recipe. What is the English recipe for the Welsh? Watkins offers his own face in the mirror. Fortunately, Watkins and his fellow Thatcherites are now out in the open where everyone can see them for what they are: philistines and proud of it. They are proud to be an isolated minority. They are proud of their hostility to the Arts. Now they have the power to destroy the Arts in both our countries. That's what I meant when I said that Watkins shames me as a theatre-lover.

This split between the Watkinses and the world is consistent. Your plan was not treated with universal contempt, only with Watkins's contempt. (Of course Watkins, like Thatcher, sees himself as a whole universe!) As the record proves, your Plan was received with courtesy and gratitude as a useful and timely stimulant. What a good idea to re-issue the Plan in your Black Book so that people can always refer to it. Again, your approach is to blame: you keep making everything public! Such decisions about policy should be taken in strictest secrecy!

But did Watkins deign to read your Plan? Presumably he considers it beneath his contempt. After all, he was only the director of a theatre in Wales who professed "a genuine desire to produce new works," although he is not not Welsh himself.

Anyone who does take the trouble to read the Plan, or your Stage articles (also in the Black Book --what an accumulation!) cannot fail to be struck by the sincerity of your purpose. Suggestions for improving the theatre you so clearly love, in the land you clearly love, come sparking off every line. Yet they all derive from one central aim: a Welsh Theatre. It is, as you put it, simple. Such simplicity must be as frustrating as it is comforting.

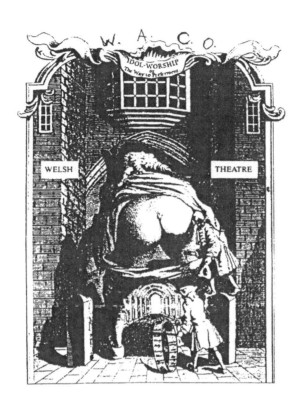

IDOL-WORSHIP
or THE WAY TO PREFERMENT IN THE THEATRE IN WALES.
First issued in the 1730s - the practice followed assiduously ever since.

Of the hord of proposals (a Central Office of
Information for Welsh theatre, fixed terms and rules for
all appointees, accountability, contracts to graduates
from the Welsh College of Music and Drama, the use of

professionals and experts in the Welsh Arts Council, the abolition of specific abuses in bursaries, grants and awards and loads more) - Watkins says nothing! Of the play competition, backed by worthwhile prizes – Watkins says nothing! Of the GB Shaw statement of principle – Watkins says nothing! Of the four seasons offering twenty-eight Welsh plays - Watkins says something! He spots that one of these twenty-eight plays is by Dedwydd Jones! Shock horror! All Watkins can see is Vanity. Everything in the Plan is a smokescreen. It is a huge conspiracy designed to sneak in plays by that scoundrel. Isn't a play about Twm O'r Nant, the father of Welsh drama, central to the aim? Certainly. But we don't want that aim. All Watkins can see is that the play is by a playwright who should be banned. Who *was* banned in the theatre Watkins controlled for four years. He gloats about that. Are your plays automatically banned? For Watkins, certainly they are. Watkins openly insists they ought to be banned not only from Wales but from the world. Why? There must be something powerful in them to provoke such a reaction! Of course there is: it is precisely the cultural tradition which is exemplified by Twm. If Watkins bans your work, would he ban the whole tradition? Certainly! Thanks to this clear admission of policy, everyone can now understand why Welsh plays are banned from theatres in Wales. If they wouldn't believe you, they have only to listen to Watkins.

Under the Watkins policy, people like you deserve only silence or exile. Which means you forfeit your Welsh ness - in his eyes! A Welshman in exile ceases to be Welsh but an Englishman in Wales is Welsh - the

140

man's an idiot! Was he laughed out of Wales? His views cannot be defended by reason, but they never pretended to be based on reason --only on prejudice. His policy is designed to keep all Welsh culture in exile. Instead, a fake Welsh culture will be imported which is neither Welsh nor culture. To what extent is Watkins voicing his own views and how far are they official policy? Thanks to Watkins the public can now see through another lie. The claim "if there is any new talent, it isn't knocking on my door!" was never meant to be taken seriously. Once more it is noticeable that the "Welsh" is omitted! The search for "new talent," like the "new work" loved by Watkins, is to establish the famous "broadly-based Welsh theatre." In plain English, this means **not Welsh.** They would reply it shouldn't be **exclusively** Welsh. Instead it should be "international," which is only a pretext for denying "national" (i.e. Welsh) plays. So they end up with an exclusively Welsh range.

Watkins is not alone. The famous "closed door" statement was made by another theatre administrator, Roger Tomlinson. It was in the Western Mail, no less. Look for yourself, in March of last year. New talent knows what to do when the door is firmly slammed in its face. Either it goes elsewhere or it kicks down the door! The directors of theatres in Wales know very well how many people are trying to kick down their doors. The noise is loud enough to be heard in England. Your articles in The Stage put on record that a whole culture is knocking. Of course your exposure of this scandal have made you a scapegoat. I suspect you knew this would happen. Just as you knew that given enough rope, the Watkinses and Tomlinsons would hang themselves -

in public. I see I've got carried away! But I feel it was worth putting the record straight. Somebody in England had to stand up and be counted. I'm afraid we were so busy with the Frankfurt Book Fair and moving house that we missed the chance to write to The Stage. Still, as long as you know there are some people this side who know what is being done in their name. It will all be a memory one day, the sooner the better, and Welsh plays will come from their native theatres to England. Then there will be no more dykes and we will all laugh at the

notion that it was ever otherwise.

John Nicholson, Bedford, England

Letter to Dedwydd Jones, Nov 3rd, 1981

### Monopoly

SIR, - On my last visit to a "Welsh" theatre (The Sherman), I picked up a glossy brochure announcing "Tenth Birthday Celebration!" The eight plays picked to celebrate the Sherman's ten extraordinary years were, *Faust* (Goethe); *Ghosts* (Ibsen); *Measure for Measure* (Shakespeare); *All* my *Sons* (Arthur Miller); *Farget-me-nat-Lane* (Peter Nichols); *Educating Rita* (Willy Russell); *Having* a *Ball* (Alan Bleasdale) and *The Claggies* (Bill Tidy). All were star productions, from, variously, Theatre Clwyd, Made in Wales and Theatre Wales. And all make Geoffrey Axworthy's pious pro-Welsh fictions (The Stage, August 25th) just so much transparent goo.

How could such a sublime non-Welsh list of plays come to be passed off as part of Welsh theatre celebrations? The answer, in a word, is monopoly. The directors of the main stages of Wales, and of Wales's main theatre-subsidizing body, the Welsh Arts Council (WAC), constitute an artistic and financial monopoly.

Outside of the massively supported big theatres, the smaller theatre groups (of whatever hue) are all, in WAC officialese, "under constant review." Hence the tortured manoeuvrings of the new Theatre Wales and of any other small group, to conform to the monopoly's preconceptions of the theatre, especially "safe" theatre. Hence, Geoffrey's one-off "Welsh" rip-offs –studio productions, rehearsed readings and playwrights' workshops - all meant, of course, to keep the dramatists "in their proper stations."

It was precisely because of this rotten system that the Welsh Dramatists Network was born. The problem has nothing to do with weird obsessions about terrorist-nationalists-under-the   stage-plotting-to-overthrow-the UK! It has to do, simply, with breaking, once and for all, the entrenched bureaucratic, sixteen-year Welsh theatre cartel. Until that happens, Axworthy's theatre "celebrations" will remain about as typically "Welsh" as a production of "The Cloggies" in Abadan.

Meanwhile, Happy Birthday Goethe, Ibsen, Bill Tidy, etc.

Dedwydd Jones, Lausanne, Switzerland

The Stage, September 8th, 1983

*Swansea pansy in disguise*

## Plan for Welsh Drama, Long Term

## Outline

**1.** Introduction and Analysis

**2.** Organisational Policy

**2.1.** The introduction of a policy to control artistic directors.

**2.2.** The introduction of a scheme for the promotion of Welsh dramatists.

**2.3.** The introduction of long-term theatre administration.

**2.4.** The establishment of an independent office of theatre information.

**2.5.** The establishment of schemes for jobs for Welsh theatre personnel.

**3.** The Role of the Welsh Arts Council

## 1. Introduction and Analysis

The potential for promoting indigenous drama in Wales is enormous. But this potential only exists because nothing has yet been done to exploit it. There is no "theatre" in Wales today, only theatres. The absence of a native Welsh drama is due to two causes --a preference for playhouses rather than plays, and the absence of any long-term co-ordinated plan, either at the centre (the Welsh Arts Council) or in any of the individual theatres. If the end-product of drama is plays, then the WAC and the theatres of Wales have ignominiously failed drama.

The absence of a plan accounts for the piecemeal, fragmentary quality of our theatre. There is no common policy or purpose, no co-ordination, collaboration or consultation, either at the centre or the periphery. Stop-go, confusion, debt, chaos, collapse and hostility are ubiquitous and endemic. All this must continue under the present regime and regimen.

The theatres of Wales are like in-growing toe-nails, they engender their own poisons and each is separately

145

owned. It is just as well that little contact exists between those pestilent prima donnas, the Artistic Directors. Their contagious lust for the golden cure-ails - pensions, perks, junkets, and especially state subsidised commercial hits - have contaminated many a wholesome theatre novitiate. The unclean directorial touch transforms healthy playhouses into high-risk Sanatoriums of Greed. If the directors ever acted in concert, the deadly virus *Vanitas Cupiditas Directorium* would soon bring about pretty bloody mutual annihilation.

The current confusion and ill-feeling are also the result of indiscriminate theatre building on the horse-before-the-cart principle. Once completed, the theatres become not centres of Welsh drama, but the domains of arbitrary outsiders with autocratic powers, from which there is no appeal and in which there exists little purpose but opportunism and self-aggrandisement.

The first essential, therefore, is for a clear-cut plan set within a definite time limit. Time provides continuity, and, a plan, direction. The inevitable collapse, of, for example, the Welsh Drama Company, was a direct result of such a lack. There was no plan within the WDC or at the Welsh Arts Council. Michael Geliot was appointed out of chaos, by confusion, into disaster (where chaos=WAC, confusion=Welsh Drama Company, and disaster=Geliot). However the WAC must assume the greater part of the responsibility, for Geliot was their choice in the first place.

I suggest, therefore, that the aim of the Welsh theatre be now stated unequivocally -The **Establishment of a Genuine Indigenous National** Drama - and the time to establish this aim be set at five years. (This five-year plan will be outlined in detail later). I would first like to make the following recommendations, in three parts.

## 2. Organisational Policy

### 2.1. The Introduction of a Policy to Control Artistic Directors

Artistic Directors, like dramatists, must be made accountable. This can only be done by conditions of appointment. But before such conditions can be introduced, there must be a radical change in Arts Council policy. It is impossible to expect outside directors (Michael Geliot for example) to learn about Wales, her language, culture, traditions and character, in the few months preceding appointment. The WAC must learn to trust its own professionals and appoint Welshmen. All directors must be appointed for fixed periods, and for an initial maximum period of three years. The Director's brief would be plain - to give preference to Welsh writers, actors and staff, and to serve the interests of the community. Failure to fulfill this brief would result in termination of contract at the end of the initial three years. Thus, from the start there would be a plan, continuity and direction.

### 2.2. The Introduction of a.Scheme for the Promotion of Welsh Dramatists

This would involve the introduction of Welsh resident dramatists into every theatre in Wales. No plan exists in Wales, at any level, for the long-term training of dramatists, particularly if the dramatist is young. Such training can take place only in a theatre. The Welsh dramatist, as well as the Welsh director, would automatically relate to the needs of other Welsh theatre professionals, and to the Welsh community. This, in turn, would do much to establish indigenous drama, which is the object of the exercise. The dramatist would be given security of tenure for an initial period of three years. His purpose would be to write plays for "his" theatre. Any failure on his part would result in the termination of his contract at the end of the three-year period. This scheme, too, would be inexpensive, for it is cheaper to establish native drama by means of single dramatists than by a multiplicity of costly theatres. It would also eradicate those unseemly public disputes involving the front-line troops of the theatre, the dramatists.

### 2.3. The Introduction of Long-term Theatre

Administrators

In view of the often ephemeral nature of directorial tenure, it is necessary that theatres have at least one permanent theatre officer. This would be the Chief Administrator, who would be appointed on a long-term basis, with clear-cut non-artistic duties. He would provide both the continuity and business and administrative stability. The Administrator would also be the permanent adviser on costs and finance to any new director, be his guide to the theatre and a bridge to the community.

*Swansea Council on a nipple hunt*

## 2.4. The Establishment of an Independent Office of

Theatre Information

The aim of such a body would be the promotion of professional drama in Wales. It would be an impartial collecting house for all theatre administration, and all such information would be freely given, on request. It would inventory technical equipment available for loan or exchange. It would co-ordinate play programmes, seasons and dates, and all professional schemes, from street theatre to opera. It would act as a job agency for all Welsh theatre personnel. It would be a comprehensive information pool available for all and would exist solely to serve the theatre. In Cardiff, for example, there are a dozen theatre organisations within walking distance of each other. It is a sad fact that no planned collaboration exists between them. The aims of such a body would be unequivocal, and the period of its

149

initial work could be set at five years (or a given shorter period). It would have purpose, continuity and direction.

## 2.5. The Establishment of Schemes for Jobs for Welsh

Theatre Personnel

This would involve planning the recruitment of Welsh theatre personnel, and afterwards of securing jobs for them in Welsh theatres. It is absurd, for example, that no co-ordinated scheme exists for arranging jobs for graduates of the Welsh College of Music and Drama. These graduates should be given preference and put under one-year contracts. This would serve as an invaluable introduction to professional life in the theatre. Such recruitment into Welsh theatres would also include technicians, carpenters, front of house staff --in short, all theatre jobs. Such job information could be compiled by the Theatre Information Office. This scheme would also eradicate the English provincial aspect which so many of our theatres now present. Again, such a scheme would possess continuity and direction.

## 3. The Role of The Welsh Arts Council

### 3.1. Re-arrangement

The 1978 proposals to reform the Welsh Arts Council, came, of course, after the English Arts Council's declared intention of instituting similar internal reforms. London aimed to "democratize" the appointment of its own officials, possibly by election. At its highest level, too, London intended to de-politicize its members. The Welsh Arts Council was duly impressed. Its own grandiose "Court of Governors" has long been a dumping ground for faithful party hacks appointed from the Welsh Office. These "governors" are part-time (one year) and amateur. One of them is quoted thus, "We don't want the dead hand of professionalism here!" If future appointments are to become elective, they must be, of necessity, professional and from bodies connected with the Arts. They ought to be long-term (at least three years), payment must be adequate, the numbers limited and the committee rules (quorums, for example) clear cut.

(Non-attendance should carry penalties, the ultimate being dismissal). Similar reforms, too, need to be carried out in the other departments of the WAC. The fact that there are no quorums on the WAC's committees leads to totally unfounded accusations of wire-pulling, manipulating, fixing, favouritism, partiality, discrimination and bias.

Finally, without radical reform, the Present Errors and Hostilities are bound to continue.


### 3.2. The Present Bursaries and Awards System

The Pauper's Charter System is clearly designed to promote cliques, coteries and discord by a very obvious system of universal disqualification depending on the whim of the awarding body and on the "good behaviour" of the applicant. This baleful and pernicious system must be scrapped forthwith. It is at the root of the hostility which exists between the administrators of the Arts and the artists themselves.

### 3.3. The Immediate Cessation of Awards to Foreign Nationals

This must be done in order to supress Continental junketings on the part of the Awarding body, and to curtail squalid overseas displays of Welsh parochial vanity which only serve to bring the WAC, and Wales itself, into contempt and ridicule.

### 4. The Five-Year Plan

### 4.1. Programme

If the end product of drama is plays, then our theatres have failed Welsh drama. Our dramatists have NOT, as is shown by the long lists of still unproduced Welsh plays. The establishment of an indigenous drama rests, first, upon the productions of the following Welsh plays, over a suggested period of five years (or shorter) by Welsh performers and directors.

SEASON ONE (Five plays) *Taffy* by Caradoc Evans; *Change* by JO Francis; *A Comedy of Good and Evil* by Richard Hughes; one foreign classic and one English piece of the same period.

### SEASON TWO (Seven plays)

*Under Milkwood* by Dylan Thomas; *Progress to the Park* by Alun Owen; *House of Cowards* by Dannie

Abse; *Small Change* by Peter Gill; *Bard* by Dedwydd Jones; one foreign and one English play of the same period. The first two seasons would take place over a period of two years or less. This season would run simultaneously with the other schemes already outlined. Before the start of the first season, the whole five- year plan (or less) would be announced and a major new play competition launched at the same time. The competition would offer substantial cash prizes and a guarantee of production to all winners. (Money in hand and the promise of performance are the sharpest spurs to any dramatist).

### SEASON THREE (Eight plays)

This season would consist entirely of new plays written for the major competition.

### SEASON FOUR (Eight plays)

This season would be devoted to new plays, not only by Welsh authors, but by any foreign or English-writing dramatist of any nationality.

### SEASON FIVE

This season would be a culmination of the Five-Year Plan. It would consist of a selection of the most successful productions of the first four seasons. The outcome of the fifth season would be unequivocal --the establishment of a Welsh indigenous drama.

**4.2.** Artistic Policy

This is embodied in George Bernard Shaw's article on Welsh Drama which appeared in the South Wales Daily Post on June 13th,1914.

### 4.3. Conclusion

The above plan is a suggested outline. However, the overall aim is clear --the establishment in Wales of an indigenous national drama, based on the principles of continuity, direction, logic and nationality. That is all.

### Footnote

This plan was originally circulated to all relevant bodies in September 1978.

# BLACK BOOK ON
# THE WELSH THEATRE
# VOLUME II

## IS LOST TO THE WORLD

*Typical Wog Bard (circa 1987) - still cheerful after 50 years of tramping round the Welsh theatres*

**The Black Books - Viewpoints:**

"Will have you laughing hysterically or fuming with rage."

Cwmbran Checkpoint

"Spares few blushes."

Liverpool Daily Post

"Repugnant and sinister...a pen dipped in blood and acid."

Morning Star

"Nobody has fought harder for a dignified, lively and honourable theatre in Wales than Dedwydd Jones."

Jan Morrys

"Pervaded by chauvinism of the most bizarre and nauseous kind...would make the National Front pale into reasonableness...yet another example of the cock-eyed misinformation from this expatriate Welshman who is the most ill-informed outsider of them all."

Graham Watkins, theatre director

"The first cuckoo in Spring."

Geoffrey Axworthy, theatre director

---

## WARNING!

153 year old pesky dramatist D.J. is on a tour of the 'Principality' - as they still quaintly call the area. DJ loves the non-pareil theatre folk of Wales, such lovable rogues (see above): 'The Colossus of the Short Stemmed Pipe,' 'Three Thousand Acres Pritchardo,' 'Geoffrey (very late) Ostrich-Egg Axworthy,' 'Councillor Jockstrap Lewis - the Man with the Cleanest Mind in the World, 'Roger Jargoneer Tomlinson,' 'Clive Whirling Dervish Barnes and many more. What have they been up to? View their plaques! Reel at their outstanding uterances! Tread in their Malodorous Pastrures! - characters and places you will never forget, all in Black Books III, IV and V!! Hi there! ! And more to come!

Pritchardo tightens up the WACO ship and squelches the Turd in High Places

# BLACK BOOK ON THE WELSH THEATRE, VOLUME III

## (1985-1987)

## "D 0 L LOP S"

*a review in one act*

**CAST**

**TAFF** - *Welshman*

**DREADLOX** - *West Indian*

**NOBBY** - *Cockney*

**WACOCHAP** - *Anglo-Welsh Snob*

**WACO** - *Welsh Arts Council*

The play can be performed by four actors, or as a monologue by one actor using different accents, as indicated.

*(**TAFF**, as Introducer, stands at a small table. He looks up from piles of paper in front of him - his 'Review'. His accent changes to stage-Welsh whenever indicated in the text.)*

**TAFF**: In these last two years our nice Welsh theatres, our fine Funding Bodies, Committees, Councillors, Organizers, Minor Officials and Major Parasites, have offered, in high Moral Tones, the most Uplifting Prayers for our hopes to come in these Hard Arted Times. All declared solidarity, yet again, with the Aged, the Crippled, the Blind,the Worthless and the Top Salaried. The Welsh Arts Council, *'WACO',* cried out for still more Moral Stances, Community Commitment and Continuing Increments. They were echoed by their bloated satellites, the WACO Luxury Leech Farms: the Grand of Swansea, the Sherman of Cardiff, the Torch of Milford and, Paradigm of them all, Toby-OBE's *(pronounced 'Oby')* Palace at Robertson, Mold. Over now to Taffo-Thicko Number One for first, and - hopefully last, impressions. *(Accent changes to stage-Welsh)* Indeed now, it was the State of Decency on the Stages of Swansea that our Councillors was most dead perturbed about. Councillor *'We-want-to-be-famous'* Lloyd whined rightly that on the Grand's panto poster "the Council wasn't even mentioned". He demanded "equal billing" because "the Council was paying".

(Thought the taxpayers were, Councillor!) Never mind, the Fame Lobby won the day. The extremely Worshipful Mayor - fair play! - revealed what it was to be respectable, and the Council duly became famous.

Then there was this Pretty Pictures Crisis. An artist's impression of the six (or eight or twelve or whatever) million pound Grand refurbishments which showed Swansea's elite foyer folk swannin' round in flash evenin' dress. (Decor was "1920's ice-cream parlour" when Taff Penguins and their ladies was tops.) Councillor, once *'Intrepid',* Evans rhapsodied: 0, lovely it is again "to dress up to go to the theatre" 'cos, see, there was now "a feel of grandeur" round "the jewel in our theatre crown". Organizer Trevor Owen done his credo proper: "No hi-tech shock here! We will be classical - far from brash!" and the roof was raised, and I means quite literal! Welsh virtue, too, became flesh in the person of world-renowned Councillor Richard *'Jockstrap'* Lewis. Done his lewd homework a treat! Researched "back through the licences 'til 1929" a.nd discovered that "plays that didn't serve the community" was torn in half and hung on a string in the toilet. (0, Antique Virtue Triumphant!) How our dear Dick loathes them filthy poofs! Dick's noble watchword: "Re-criminalize homos!" With you, Jockstrap, I'll go all the way! See, ordinary troubled Tories been accostin' Dick right out there in the streets itself, mutterin': "We are all behind you!" Watch it sailors, Jockstrap's on the Vice Squad!

Two years previous, rejoice I did, Councillor Dick banned them *Romans* buggerin' round Britain. (Hear! Hear! Show me buggery and I'll show you "immoral

161

acts"!) Now Jockstrap got roused up by "the male relationships" in *That'll Be The Day* and *All Fall Down* - the first ever "clear-eyed look" at TaffAids. (But not a glimpse of it, will you be gettin', you sweaty, palm-tufted, smutty-minded Swansea boyos!) "This is nota homosexual exercise," author A. Heritage swore breathlessly.

"Nobody as much as takes a sock off!" gasped Organizer Dennis Downes. (Tell that to the Marines, boys! Swansea's had enough of these Dirty-Knob Plays!) Councillor Dick *knows* Swansea "has more than its fair share of gay problems". (How's he know that, then!?) Watch those flies!

There was also this justifiable fewroar over this repulsive *Stags And Hens* play by this *Theatre of Bad Odours* (Ha! Ha!) "set in a ladies' and gents' " with soiled towels, sodden paper and dull plumbing done "in authentic detail". Then in come another Low Company, *Black Door* with its Four-Letter-Word Play *Tramps,* about "the most hideous sexual murders in the entire history of the universe, seen through the eyes of a tramp". Who wants tramps on stage, I asks? Didn't we have *Romantic Comedy* on before that? And who got buggered then? But banned we got the Mayfair Club's *Electric Video Road Show's* Topless Models! Don't them beastly erect old nipples provoke just as much "sexual assaults"? Stiffer penalties against sex pests is all Swansea Councillors wants to behold! And, happy to report, our perfect righteousness now also applies to tainted films. Teacher Grant *'Indignation'* Williams ordered his schoolboys out of a Swansea cinema after "Howard, an obscene, erotic unsuitable duck" felt-up girl ducks in whirlpools and, worse, did "acts of blasphemy". o, why, I asks, is turns like *The Anarchic Cabaret of the Mad Kiwi Ranter* so popular in Swansea? But in spite of Councillor Dick's fine upstanding campaign, there was some nasty climaxes. No use dodgin' it. One bad one was at Adelaide Street's *Marina Nite Spot* - and physically perilous as morally catastrophic it was! Shameful to say, our own esplanade matrons, some age-old grandma pensioners even, "behaved like animals" *(The Stage,* December 19,1985). Nude *male* strippers done it this time! One "dressed as a schoolboy" and the other as *The Gladiator* in "a Spartacus-type outfit". Watch that Spartacus, Jockstrap! 'Cos when he peeled off "it whipped (!) the ladies into a frenzy". And when he offered them baby oil to rub on his botty he got dragged off the stage. (It was at this point that "the respectable element" in the audience "hid themselves behind pillars".) Thc Management finally had to act and four bouncers "returned the strippers to the stage". A bit boisterous but the ladies liked it," observed one Organizer. But now - the dirtiest, lowdown bit-part of all - the Chief Constable of Swansea, David *'The Helmet'* Jones himself, unforgivably washed his hands - the Uplands Pontius Pilot - statin' he had "no comment to make on the issue". Turncoat! Dirty devil! You listen now, Chief Constable boyo - there is not enough tea in the whole of China for you to hide in! There was, too, a silly bit of an unreal crisis over simple arithmetic gone wrong again. About this smidgeon of cash out of six million or eight or whatever, to make the Grand Theatre gloriouser. See, Grand Organizer, Paul Dyson (a spender generous but not spendthrift is my meaning). Well, some say about £l38,000 went off

163

somewhere, disappearing apparently into *Mother Goose,* never to come out again. All this in the teeth of *Care, Diligence and Skill,* a WACO "check-list" against theatre over-spending. But Swansea still made it! See, our Councillors was "too generous" with "discretion" to Paul. I mean, Councillors can always get away with budget overspending to a measly £5,000 or so. No trouble that is. But our Councillors, in their pure idea of Swansea democracy, give away too much autonomy like to Paul. To tip the winky, what it was that really drove our Councillors up the wall was when they discovered "no cloakroom had been built" and that "the carpets that had been fitted weren't the ones that had been ordered" *(Western Mail,* December 11, 1986). But then, like it does so nice in Swansea, the bother soon "normalized" itself. The £138,000 loss was "pruned back" to "£87,000" and of this "£82,000" was blamed - yes indeed - on *Mother Goose!* Anyway, 'cos of "underspending elsewhere" the Council found that it was after all really "in pocket by £250,000"! So sayin' Paul was sacked for "alleged gross misconduct and culpability" *(Western Mail,* January 9, 1987) was oversimplified, see, if not downright panicky! Not even a damn near suspicious affair it was - for Swansea. So, ladies and gentlemen, that is how Councillors and Jockstraps of Swansea keeps the Grand and the elite sm ellin, so sweet! Go on! Smell us! Well, this irresistible tide of moral Ajax spread to Cardiff, too. That foul *Black Door* and its sexual tramps was finally undone! (Already been done previous they had for pubic screw in, in *Lady Chatterly's Lover.)* Living up to its public briefs the WACO went and give those preverts and their sewage gas a month to pack their poofs and begone!

Then, 0 glory to the Right, the WACO chopped the *Action Pie Company* too. "We are the victims of a Macarthyite witch-hunt!" they frothed. Well, let me put everybody right, right now! All it was, was the five main Organizers was belongin' to that traitorous, terrorist Workers Revolutionary Party! Honest, that's all there was to it! And let me assure thOse guilty, fleein', yellow Reds, the officers of WACO are far from being "Mama Thatcher's little wankers!" They are, in fact, Swansea's! To tidy up now a few odds and sods.

We got a nice boost for our top Servile Industry, Tourism, with a first ever *Swansea* Dylan Thomas Festival, launched by the Wales Tourist Bawd - from Piccadilly! Poetry bargains at £150-£200 a week or a cut-price tenner *Dylan Thomas Birthday Weekend* was for sale. (Only they got the poet's age wrong, see, by six or sixty or whatever years. But what's the diff I ask, dead is dead and Swansea needs the bread, and dignity, right now!) Then there was the *Richard Burton Fun Run* (as opposed to the Richard, Burton Drama Award) won by John Theophilus of Swansea's own super Harriers - our city's sons showin' her healthiest side at last. Bravo there, Theo boyo! For *Annie* at the Grand they finally opted for "a daft dog", seein' as how all the others run off howlin' into the wings when the music struck up. But most adventurous was the Grand's new 4,300 foot square prestigious stage herself, where a whole mini-theatre-in-the-round for 300 was created. *One Flew Over The Cuckoo's Nest* was given, "compelling the audience to become involved in the world of a lunatic asylum"- and the whole of Wales joined in! Wheeeeee!!

*(Enter **DREADLOX**, a West Indian)*

Welcome, Dreadlox! Thought you'd never come! Your turn, sir. Report from Babylon North! Sting like a bee quite shamelessly, if you please!

**DREADLOX**: OK Taffo, man, you axed for it! Well, afta dem ten civilizin' yahs at Mold, dat Massa Georgie Roman he buggah off wid his swan-song stunna, *Waitress for the Prosecution.* (Dose top catz sure do love dat Agga Christie – she oil to their grease!) Next come in dis new Massa, Massa Toby-OBE Robertson, and den, man, t'ings get glistenin' real bright, like shit on a slate! Da fust t'ing to glittah wuz empty promises. Massa, he say dis Mold some kinda big "centre of excellence", like wid da "same cachet" (what dat, Massa?) and "on a par" (what dat, too?) "as Chichester" (where dat, Massa?). Dat Massa Tobe-OBE, he way out! He dig "Theatre of Footballs"! *(Western Mail,* October 1985.) "We're a third division team in a second division football ground." (I lost, Massa!) Toby-OBE he 'rouse dese "excellences to bring in out- side influences (like Tottenham Hotspur?) to shed life (football?) on the area." 0, dose gorgeous glimmerins! Massa, he goin' conneck Mold wid "Great Britain at large" so he "build up prestige". 0, de Lord Jeezus, how we Taffswazies wid our natural rhythms needs dat manna, man! Massa boast he "no boaster" by "burgeoning" dat Mold. (Burgeoning rna black jackass, Massa!) "Mold", dis preacha say, "is ripe for artistic face-lift", so "the right products are coming" to carry dis noble savage asshole up to "wider

166

horizons" in dat Massa Hall of Pale Face Fame! 0, bless us pore primitive Taffswazies down here in dis wog-bog! Patronize us like crazy wid yore humble civilizin' mission! Massa, like dat noble Roman before you, take up dis Taffman's burden! Shine your Angel Light on us! Toby-OBE, he some shitty big fighta, too! Wid one hand he take on dese wicked pesky Hacko-Wacos in their den, and Massa done slam dem in da bollox! Lissan! Massa, dat ferocious, say "We have no pump-priming cash!" Massa, he love dat cash! He love dose pumps! And he love dem compound adjectives! Den, like lion, he roar dose W ACOS was "minor in standards"! Pygmy, Massa! Like dat piddlin' ten-letter alphabet you even now abuses! Massa den outright condemn dis silly, sad old "Welsh factionalism". But I say dat only 'cos dey pore motha-fucka Taffies got you up dey ass, Massa! Den Massa call for "real feathers" in "artistic caps". (Dat Massa, he great poet, too!) Massa wan' dese real "caps" and "feathers" and "crowns" and "talents" all in dis fancy "forcing house" (what dat, Massa?) he got up there (fuck da theatre!). So Massa throw up "challenging atmospheres" for dis sexy-sublime Vanessa Rougetombe (who she, Massa?). 'Cos Mold jus' Massa's little old spring-bawd, I presume, into dat Theatre Protectorate of Vicomte Peter de Hall and dat luscious Baron Trevor von Fuckin' Nun! Like *Black Ice* was borned in Mold but "toured from Kendall down to Melton Mowbray" where dose Brigadiers goes when dey die. Den Massa turn modestly from da World Fame of his West End Footballs and throw in agricultures wid dis new amazin' theatre of "carrots"! (0 Massa, bard in a land of bards, you is king of the rubbish-dump line!) Dese "carrots" goin' grow in da "Green Fields of Mold".

(Let 'ern eat leeks, Massa!) But tough on Massa - dese carrots cost big shit. Massa moan he only got £900,000 and oat £300,000 too short! Massa do declare dey shitty WACOS only gives out money "in coffee spoons, never in one *dollop"*. Massa Toby- OBE - bard, fighta, friend :- you is so mighty righty! I loves dat money in dollops! Dey Taffos loves dat money in dollops! Ma black Mammy loves dat money in dollops! All God's chillun loves dai money in dollops! Da whole sickenin' human race loves dat money in dollops! And you more dan most, Massa! De whole - buggerin' history of theatre in Waaaies be 'bout dem dirty dollops and who git 'em! Den to show he love his Taffo brudders - Massa Godlike in his humility - he drag in Top Taffo-Thicko Emlyn da Williams. He get dis Emlyn namin' dat chickenshitty studio up there - "Emlyn!", like dat! He done emlyned dat Taffo-dwarfo hideaway! And Emlyn, he dat lovable he sue for peace. Den Massa (how he worship da Great Condescender in da Dress Circle of da Sky!) he look 'roun down dese Taffos here and Massa "well-pleased" 'cos he announce dey not "poor relations" no more! You rite there, Massa - for dey Taffos up dere is da most dumbest, brown-eatin', craw lin, four-legged assholes in da hole of pore wasted Welshland! Simple for Nice Lickas like Emlyn hand over own Solomon mines to Massas, 'cos dose whitie-bible-beadies tranquilize dose native stoolies and pacifies dose outside civilizin' greedies! Massa know by instink where Taffo Nice Lickas be, and if he but give da word dey Lickas dey'd gargle in der own piss!

*Dat Uncle Tom*

*He not so oldl*

*He live and well*

*And dwell in Moldl*

*Gaaaarrgi.. !*


*Buy my toothless dragons*

*Buy my Raj dollee*

*Made lor Tallo Lickas*

*In lo'burg, Anglesea!*

*Gaaaarrgi!*


To conclude dis degradin' matin', Massa insist "the situation is not black or white". Dis time, Massa, I insists you wrong - situation very black, and Massa, you very, *very* white!

NEW THEATRE

*The nearest thing to*
**HEAVEN IN WALES**

170

**TAFF**: And Welsh writers, Dreadlox boyo?

**DREADLOX:** No dollops der, man Taff. Massa put it ripey-tripey troo: "Any play by a Welsh author will be jumped on!" (Warning in letter to the Theatre Writers Union, December 5, 1986.) And from da start Massa promise dat dis Mold theatre "will give me a chance to do more *English* plays". *(Western Mail,* September 5, 1985.) Massa kep' his word. He give Barker hit *Claw; See How They Run* farce by King; *Stoppard,* night and day him! Den seein' dey Taffos all at sea, Massa go whee, whee, wheeeee! and throw up Greek *Medeas,* Irish *Translations,* Norwegian *Gabblers,* and lots 0' hot gobblin' pantos! An' what dey give you, Taff!

**TAFF**: Pisspots!

**DREADLOX**: Doubtless wid beaded bubbles winkin' at da brim, man! You no Taff Toff Licka! But why you 'gin make dese un-nice waves? Taff, I talkin' 'bout you! Dese hefty lefties in dis loony Theatre Writers Union - like Jon Preece, Carl Tighe and dat sick ilk - why you stir up dat lovely yellow broth? Up to dat time Massa Toby-OBE ignore you pen and inky pinky tatty batty weirdo wordy quillfellas! Why dese woundin' words like Toby-OBE Theatre bein' "Black Hole" for Taffscripts? 'Cos den Toby-OBE he gotta declare war! He strike back - like lead! He hire Taff Top Dreaded Champion Nice Licka, dis deadly Jeremy Brooks (Hi, fella!) and name him "dramaturge" (dat one great ugly word whatever it means!). Massa give order: "muck out dese stinky Taffscripts!" So Licka kep' yore shitpaper flyin' man. Am I right!? And enclose such fun letter (I knows!) sayin' his Massa need million dollop million times for a "change of policy". Dat Massa jus' startin' da Taff revolution wid dis *Corny Green* and Emlyn studio pigeon hole.· "Dat not much," say Licka, "but go on - laugh!" We laugh, man, like in hollow boot - hoot! hoot! hoot! Den Licka reveal he find Tafftheatrescribe deep in Dyfed Tropic Paradise, but give no name. Bravo, Licka, you got the only secret theatre writer in da world! Licka swear he got "bias" for wogwork. Yes, I say - all da way to da shreddin' machine! Licka sing, "Small nation, small scripts." I sing, "Small nation, *big shits!"* Den after all dese songs 0' self praise, da most putrid Lickas in da land, dem wobbly Welsh invertebrates of University Bangor, after all dese insuitings, dey make Massa Toby-OBE "Honorary" prophet or professor or whatever. 0 dose Top-Salaried Fuckas, dey lick each other like gay catz inn a fairy dairy! - but when it comes to Taffscribes, dey tight as a miser's ass on pay day! Love of dollops have dey like no man. I say – a plague on all their dollops! Ta ta and bye bye, fuck off and die. And let it be soon! You wan' I go on, Taff?


**TAFF:** Keep the cream on the scene, boyo!

Dramatist (30) with a tale or two to tell

**DREADLOX**: So, I'll hit the south in da mouth, den! Taff, dat Zombie Kraal, dat Sherman Leech Farm, dat place goin' from putrid to midnight! Dat ostrich-egg Organiser, Massa Axleblow, he one of da Ibadan Connection. Lissan! Dis am all da troo fax! Big Bill

Bevin, Number One Principal of dat University Cardiff, he give dat Sherman job to Axleblow. Axleblow deman' "Chair!". Big Bill say: "Just da theatre bustah!" Den Big Bill, he advertise da job, like all above bawd, 'cos they need facade of "ideal values... to save our Sherman", as Axleblow pray. But dose shitty students, dey raid Big Bill's home mansion, steal dose juicy letters and publish dat steamin' crapola all ovah da Capital of Wales. Glory! Glory! Dat yahs back. At last come dis January and all dat Senate of University is finally pissed off wid dose Ibadan Turds, and vote wid big majority "No Confidence" in Big Bill, and deman' all dollops to Sherman cut at once! Axleblow, he shrivel like scrotum on ice, 'cos on dese Leech Farms dollops be in da very air dey breathes, so if dat lollipop tree get cut, dey Massas, dey all falls down. Now Axleblow, he sob dis loss of dollops, and explain dis mean "no modern" Axleblow, no "middle-scale" Axleblow, "no other" Axleblow in all Cardiff! If Axleblow go dark, dat "devastating" for whole ofAxleblow, and "that is it"! If "axe fall" on Axelblow, it "stands as folly *forever!*" Jeezus, dat terrifying! 'Cos we needs you, Massa, like we needs a Leech Farm in our beds! Why, Cardiff without Axleblow, dat like snot without nose! And dat unimaginabubble! Axleblow, of course, rave 'gainst dose fackin' WACOS. Say WACOS play "ducks and drakes" (like 'Howard', man?) wid Sherman. (Axleblow, he great poet, too!) He salute Sherman, dis "Flagship of the Principality" - home of all the Licka wogbards in the land! But I hear other wogbards sing different tune - like "Sink dat reekin' Ibadan Hulk, 0 Senate bright, so we can breathe shite-free air again!"

Das it, Taff. Over to you!


**TAFF**: Where's Nobby, Dreadlox? It's his turn now!


**DREADLOX**: Let's kick dose pricks around 'til Nobby come, man, and when he come we kick 'em round some more!


**TAFF**: OK then. Over it is to the Tame Taff West; to Milford and its Torch, where Les *'Foot-in-both-Camps'* Miller went and handed in his dollops. (Just forgot to cancel his long-standing London reservation!) After Brigadier Watkins's narrow escape in Spring of '82 or 'three or 'four, Les's goin' come as no surprise, see, 'cos hard it is to find even a Taffo-Thicko to live in that vanishing point by the sea, with all its teeming worthies. Ashen-faced Les confessed: "I'm disillusioned". (But then, so was Jesus, boyol) "Those Glib and Oily Moguls of Amoco withdrew their Panto dollops!" Les wailed, "I can't make ends meet!" (But neither could William Ewart Gladstone, boyol) So Les naturally set about them punchy WACOS: "60,000 dollops isn't enough! That's 30,000 dollops too short for a 300,000-dollop house! There is no meat now left to trim!" (Another fuckin' poet, Dreadlox – this time in a butcher's shop!) The wellflogged WACOS blamed Ma Thatch, and Ma Thatch blamed the Theatre Writers Union! "They'll learn when it's too late,"Les prophesied - black as a black book! Well, I'll tell you what, Les, boyo, your "too late" can't be too soon for all the rest of us! Dreadlox, I

176

put all these crocodile weeps and toddler drivels down to total bloody bollocks mixed with too huge dollops!

**DREADLOX:** Spot on there - all along the line is neat geometry. Flush out all da angles! I means, Taff, please continue.

**TAFF**: Look at all these vast arithmetics! Who's deprived? Who's poor in Wales? Axelblow and his half million? Toby-OBE and his one or two or whatever millions? WACO *'Dodger'* Tomlinson and his freshblown two or three or whatever, from his Massas there in Whitiehall Town? And God knows how poor the Grand of Swansea is. Six, eight, ten or fourteen millions, all variously mentioned in the Press. £777,000 to run at the last count. And what about the mammoth vanity of a thirty million dollop Complex to Pritchardo and his W ACOS? Then there are these twilight, mythic "short falls", these charmin' if unconvincin' "prunings", and the shy, retirin' 35,000 dollop "miscellaneouses". Big arithmetic equals Big Greed, right!? These monstrous figures adapt to every bleedin' crisis, but one tender point no crisis ever touched - the WACO toppo salaries, which are even fuckin' Thatcher-proof! The money there's as clean as the snot up a baboon's nose. Dreadlox, I'm runnin' dry! *(He takes atape recorder out of his pocket)* Where the hell is Nobby?

**DREADLOX**: What you got der, man?

**TAFF**: This, Dreadlox, is one God-Almighty awful leak! Our Turd in High Places recorded it - 'tis precious WACO chappieson tape for all the world to cringe at.

**DREADLOX**: Jeezus! Dat fluff-stuff stop da buses, man!

**TAFF**: Listen, Dreadlox, with some awe!

(**TAFF** *can now imitate the English snobvoice on the tape or another actor can be used*)

**WACOCHAP**: Fraffly! Yes, in fraffly tip-top form, my fella WACO creepers, for we live as we crawled: without penury, without pride, and Ma Thatch's hatchet never cut us down to size! All our old toads are in place, we are a master race, and we welcome a brand new Supremo, Signor Mathew Pritchardo - jolly sound fella - Eton and Oxfordia, a modest 3,000 acres in The Vale, inherita, administrata of Agga Christie's *Mousetrap* millions. I give you Pritchardo, a man who knows his dollops!

**TAFF**: I'll turn down all that frantic lickin'sound...

**DREADLOX**: ...uick, man, quick!

Aloft! Councillor Richard Lewis - `The Man with the Cleanest Mind in the World`

**TAFF**: There! Yes, Dreadlox, new Pritchardo-Three-Thousand-Acres immediately switched over to the very offensive: "We will be bold... we will give a lead... we will boost the Arts... " Why these overwhelming verbal thrusts? I hear you ask - because Wales was "dropping down the (arts) ladder, rung by rung". *(Western Mail,* August 19, 1986.) (Good Lord, Dread10x, is there no end to these poet chappies, what?!) So, Pritchardo *'Three-· Thousand'* vowed he'd "follow the public... who vote with their feet" until "international recognition" was achieved! ; A damn fine line to nowhere, and no one uttered a squeak! Tight-lipped, Pritchardo then took a public oath to squelch our Turd in High Places who'd leaked *"Priorities into Practice"* to a consterpated nation. Who'd caused "red faces" in WACO toilets, and who'd provoked those bloody arts riots outside St Fagan's Folk Museum. Behind "closed door" sessions, Pritchardo hammered out new security laws and orders as yet unknown to the toiling masses. The WACO "ship" was "tightened-up", solid as a dried-out cow-pat! Never again would WACO be a "whipping boy"! (Lovely bag of droppings there, Pritchardo, first-rate WACO images!) Wales's "disgruntled", from Be1fastto Lausanne, were silenced! But damn these public communication organs - as turncoat as a Swansea Top OOp! Our "national" (hah!) daily *The Western Mail* gave space- quite unnecessarily - to the ridiculous gripes of Welsh POW Richard Digby Day (now Director-in-Custody, Players Theatre, Belfast): "Cardiff is the saddest city in Britain for live theatre." (What a whopper!) "Whenever I go back to Cardiff, I despair." (0, these bitter, absentee critics, languishing in outposts of Empire, eating their hearts out - lovely!) "The Welsh

180

Arts Council is impossible... they have the oddest ideas." (Just far beyond you, fella!) "Apart from the Chapter Arts Centre, you can forget it! (And you, too, Corporal!) And how did the W ACOS respond to this raving madman? Listen, now, to WACO Champion Jargoneer, Rodger *the Dodger* Tomlinson, at his amazing fluffiest! (TAFF *imitates upper-class English accent)* "Huge expansions... have broken box office records," because "patterns of theatre here don't replicate cities in England."

**DREADLOX**: Dose low blows! Dat "replicate". Ugh!

**TAFF**: "Wales is in the mainstream, mainstream ..." (how Roger loves his mainstreams)"... for realistic funding."

**DREADLOX**: OK! All is forgiven. Dey won dat round, words down! No come-back to dat! No helpin' it, we is all victims of discrap-trap.

**TAFF**: Here's more Pritchardo: "Fraffly funny! Haw! Haw! I say, listen, chappies, to these silly-billy anaemics of this Theatre Writers Union! Haw! Haw! So 'we possess unfettered privilege' do we, and we're 'not subject to democratic control' are we?! Haw! Haw!" Them bland choruses of "so bloodywell-whats?" and "hear hears!" - sheep in wolves' clothing, but Pritchardo's bonny brayings beat them all!

Dramatist (30) outside WACO offices contemplates a funny future

**WACOCHAP**: Haw, haw! So we're "highhanded, secretive and autocratic" too? 0 these blushing, boy-scouty-louties, wet behind the ears! - of course we are, and have been for nineteen lush, delicious and unprincipled years! *(Reads)* Bleats for "devolution!" now. Lefty obscenity scum! Special Branch trash-cans are full of such pathetic confetti! Calls for "root and branch reform"? What naive tots and twits! Ta for the laugh, I suppose. These niagaras of dollops are for the exclusive control of only indisputably top-drawer True-Blue privateers! My dear fella travellers, lavish to a man, bravos all round, our gravy train is Tory and White - we are Cardiff's One Thousand Year Reich! And Herr Supremo Pritchardo is proof against all Reform! But a sop for democracy's face! "Theatres should now use contracts with writers!" How about that!? It's a disgrace! Haw! Haw! Nineteen years too late! Up to now the Leech Farms "paid what they liked" - if they felt like it at all! Haw! Haw!

**DREADLOX**: Man, afta dat I wouldn't go for a pee in a Welsh theatre without a contract!

**WACOCHAP**: And, my fella-chappies, we've made our dollops anyway! If we ever have to run, our golden handshakes will be fun!

**TAFF**: Hoots and jeers! As per normal for writers under consideration. And that's it!

**DREADLOX**: What Pritchardo do after dat Digby Day bit?

**TAFF**: Flim-flammed all opposition with a drive "for innovative ideas" and a "Theatre Initiative Support Scheme". (Or Bring-meHungry- People's-dollops-too.) A WACO plan to "float a lottery" (what's WACO then?) sent the rest scurrying for cover! Propaganda for fools, Dreadlox, but they swallowed it whole. Finally Pritchardo stooped into the breach to release the foulest-smelling smoke-screen since Bhopal. He "threw down a gauntlet" for a 30 million dollop Performing Arts Centre in Cardiff (Old Pritchardo got a nifty Fame Game goin', too!) 40,000 dollops immediately for a "design brief' - from Bath! Then Pritchardo topped the lot with a Pronouncement outshining all other WACO gems! Pritchardo's Golden WACODOME would attract hordes - "*our cultural riches... acting as fly-paper*". Twenty thousand years of Celtic civilization reduced to sticky ends for dead flies.

**DREADLOX**: A joke of strenius from On High!

*(Enter* **NOBBY**, *a cockney)*

**TAFF**: Nobby! At last! Where you been?

**NOBBY:** In Wiles I thought, mite. Might be wrong there, tho', with all these upperclass, sugar-plum-fairy gits around - Toby-aBE, Axleblow, Dodger Tomlinson, Les Flicker the Torch, Three-Thousand Pritchardos. Toffee-nose gibber-jabber - ripe old Tory Conference cocktail night! I got lost! I mean, where was Wiles in Wiles? Where's the Taffos, the troupers, the hoofers? Jumped-up bunch of la-dedah cobblers! When I asked 'em for an audition they told me to try the tradesmen's entrance - in England! Crappy pony wankers! Court, tit, title, Pip and SirStroke Orrificer themselves up, they do.

Like this new theatre smellin' rank, a "dramatra... dramatur... turg... "


**DREADLOX:** Nobby, no disgust in' eleven letter words in here!


**NOBBY:** Hey, Dreadlox, know the diff between Stratford Avon and Stratford East? Well, the Avons say "fraffly" and we say "fackin", and "fackin's" fackin' English, mite! Yeh! Piss up all their sleeves, say we theatre workin' men! And Taff, I seen you got a different lingo here. A real langwidge sandwich, mite, verbs and all. Bleedin' insult exportin' all our dummies and semi-literates here! Get us a bad nime all over Wiles. Should learn the Queen's fackin' English before they opens their smartie-traps. Like this 'igh and Mighty Axleblow when I called in. Listen! "If the axe falls... on the momentum... "


**DREADLOX:** I begs yah, Nobby, let it not fall outa thy mouth!

**TAFF**: He still got the dry heaves from the last bag of officialese. All right, Dreadlox?


**DREADLOX**: Who can escape the terrible sentence of WACO manure?! OK, Nobby, go on. Back on rna knees now.

**NOBBY**: For them Massas O' yours, Dreadlox lad, it's Apocalypse Now! Listen to Axleblow *(imitates upper-class accent):* "There will be no second chance after the taking away of the stage from beneath the feet."

**DREADLOX**: Man, what *did* keep you? Not dose verbal slimies.


**NOBBY**: Looking for a Welsh play, I was. I mean, me gran rna seen *The Mousetrap. The Corn Was Green* in her youth. *Hair* when I was in tiddIy-winks. *Oliver* in me nursery. *Joe Egg's* a bit long in the tooth. *Piafs* from France. *Catch* 22 _:- I was a squaddie, too. *Jayne Air's* sixth-form library, so's *The Black Hill.* Why so many -novels? Well, corner them dollops! Out of copyright's a gift. Adaptors' fees, Directors' fees, Translators' fees, taxi and transfer fees! Fat rackets from older versions! Not an original scribe in sight. (Which is the whole point!) *When Did You Last See Your Trousers?* Was Antrobus. *Murder in the Red Barn,* Victorian. *Canterbury Tales* from the Peasants' Revolt. *Looking For The World* by a Taff (definitely) - Edwards, but all about Greece! *The Man Born to be Hanged* (at last!) was Dick Hughes at hisbest. But that was in another country and, besides the man is dead! Then all these imported Organic One Night Stands: Wheat-Germ Interludes (by Aries); Whale Soliloquys (by Belgrano); Palestinian oneliners out of Aborigine Skits; Pinochet Double-Take Diet-Tribes; Condom Park and Hunchback Dramas in Down-TownLos Angeles; Keep the Pope off the Moon! *Anything* as long as it's very far away! All fer yer Hand-job Hampstead Trendies on Supplement-Worshippin' weekends in Wiles. No wonder their second cottages gets burned away! Wot about *entertainment* plays for evr'ybleedin'body ev'rybleedin'where, me old mities?!

**TAFF**: Bring back the Gladiators!

**NOBBY**: Fit 'em in, no trouble. Omelette Prince of Egg; Dunlop, Prince of Tire; Tony and Cleo. As you like its, what you wills. Tons of homogenized Roman Shakesburts here. (Don't tell Jockstrap, tho'!) Wot's made it in London, they put in museums! Poncing-off-the-dead-in-posh-accents-drama's a terrible sight! So, all right, our Shakesburt can write them lovely true words over all his work, "All me own. work". Right, but give your Taff Shakesburts a chance! I mean, howdid Bill get *his* start? (But Shakesburt's just perks for those upper-class jerks and their monocled fackin' egos!) Not like Mike James of the *not* Made in Wales Company, wot couldn't "imagine openin'a new company without Shakesburt". Taff, I gotta say it - you got more Nice Lickers here than slugs on buttercup benders on wet afternoons! Itsa frutty-tutty pisspot wherever yer looks!

**DREADLOX**: Gaaaarrgl... !!! Dose piss-green bubble blowers!

WACO official in unaccustomed genial mood

**NOBBY**: This Gilly Adams Sherman Leeches again - swears there's "no flow of scripts... no tradition of professional writing in drama, for radio or theatre in Wiles"! But Dick Hughes wrote the first radio play in the world, and Dylan the best! And Twm O'r Nant made a pile in Brecon in '84 (an' I means 17 *(seventeen)* Adrian *'BBe'* Mourby wrote them Lickas was "more interested in plays from England than Wales". And Adrian's from England, Licka Gilly! "No flow of scripts"! A likely Lady! Spot that dodge! They gotta keep talent away 'cos talent would stand out a mile and they'd sink outta fackin' sight! If the talent I seen in Wiles was ever encouraged in Wiles, them Lickas would go "wheeee!" out of their tiny dollops and those colonized Leech Farms would go free! But can't have that,can we? So, it's always "no flow of scripts".

**DREADLOX**: What they really got, Nobby, is dat stinkin' dried pukepuke of mediocrity all ovah dah face.

**NOBBY**: Spot on! Yellow is yellow wherever the egg. Of course there's a "flow of scripts" (and script writers) - but to England. Frank *'Rhondda'* Vickery hired a London theatre to put on his play – his only chance in Wiles! All *his* own work, and not favoured on your Leech Farms! And Frank's got another in Oldham soon. Colin Mason's got *Changes* at the Lyric, Hammersmith, where Richard Hughes got his start. That still leaves Dannie Abse, Gwyn Thomas and Caradoc for starters or afters, mite! Met Sion Mathias of Swansea just after he wowed them in Soho just after he wowed them in

189

Edinburgh. "I love Wales," he said, "but getting a play on takes two years of your life." Blimey, Sion, Caradoc took fifty in Wiles, so stick with it here! All the Taff actors I met in Stratford- a d I mean East - say the same. Paul *(Absolute Beginners)* Rhys: "I'd love to work in Wales. I think it's a disgrace we don't have something like the Glasgow Citizen's Theatre. I'll set up my own Company. It's my home. There was no theatre in Neath in my day." Well, Paul, mite, there still ain't nowhere from what I just seen! Karl *(Jesus Christ Superstar)* Johnson: "I don't get a chance to honour my roots. I'd love to come back and work in Wales." Taff Director Ceri Sherlock, like Digby Day, had a bash. Saidhis departure from Wales was "a reflection of the artistic climate in Wales and the Welsh Arts Council, who are more interested in saving buildings than people". Ceri promised "to import Welsh talent" when he's in London, Amsterdam or New York. All in all, Taff, I gotta say it, but you got one fackin' ripe-monumental cock-up down here.

**TAFF**: Agreed, my noble Nobby!

**NOBBY**:. Well, wot you gonna do about it, Taff?

**DREADLOX:** Yeah, man, and can we help?

**TAFF**: Boyos, I want you to listen to this leaked celebratory splurge of WACOS in full session - then I think, my merry fellow scribes, you'll know exactly what I'm going to do!

Typical Welsh theatre script receptacle (late 20th Century)

**WACOCHAP**: Fraffl! Fraffl! These penpushing paper ruffians! What fun would our Council be without them! *You* have all no doubt heard these bookish black rumours around. *You* will ignore them! They are not a piggish smear campaign, except against themselves! No twisted complaints have been sent to Editors and MPs at any time whatever from any source! Not one of us here can be blamedfor one jot of anything! WACO club membersare as unblemished as hell! And why,chappies? Simply, basically, because those Union scribblers would never dare tell this so-called "stinking truth" of theirs. Because it does not exist and, if it did, they wouldn't know it. And, if they did and told it, no one would believe it. For what it concerns is a matter holy to every normal human on planet earth - a matter of thick, steaming, juicy, top-dog dollops, which represents the Highest Principle and Ultimate Morality for all faithful WACOS and their Satraps, Worthies, Leeches and Nice Lick ers, and there are plenty of those around! "For what we areabout to receive, again and again and again, may the Lord make us truly thankful." 0, must Press Release that one! Lordy, Lordy, what a hoot! So I do vehemently, and with the most utter confidence, reassure you, not one of these Theatre Union ink-stained scruffs will dare even try tell this ridiculous so-called "truth"! *Ever!* So, Supremo Pritchardo, how about pink gins all round for your chummy chum chums?!?

**CURTAINS**

# BLACK BOOK ON THE WELSH THEATRE VOLUME IV

### (1988-1990)

## *'Asides'*

Officers of WACO after visiting a Dedwydd Jones play

*(ENTER PLAYWRIGHT, dressed as the Tramp (30) in the above illustration. Waves to audience)*


*PLAYWRIGHT: Hello everyone, everywhere. Yes, well, now I am in my hundred and fifty third year, I can look back on the old dramas of life with a certain detachment, if not amusement. So when I was invited recent by the Anarchist Society of the New Confederation of European States to record my memories of the Welsh Theatre between 1986 and 1989, and beyond, I laughed out loud – like that - ha, ha! When I'd recovered, I gladly agreed. I also undertook to conduct a tour cum commentary through the swamp... er... 'Park' of Welsh Theatre Remembrance with its massy monuments to the glorious Arts Prominents of our past. All in Black Books III, IV, and V, dead ahead.*


The Welsh Arts Council Museum (W ACOM) which stands at the entrance to the Park, is a stunning example of top Welsh ruin value, with deadly nightshade and black horehound growing out of every crumbling breeze-block. Iron-wrought gates rusting in the nettles almost beyond recognition - like many a dramatist this foetid limbo was once meant to represent. The Museum also houses the fabled *Vestibule of Plaques of the Prominents* - a regurgitation really of the staggering tombs and charismatic mausoleums you see outside. The Museum also houses the sublime *Album of Welsh*

*Theatre Recollections* and its hugely entrancing sister tome the *Book of Outstanding Theatre Utterances.*

Essential dramatist's equipment (after two weeks use)

*One, two, three - piss on you, piss on me! - sorry, just testing.*

Yes, duw, when I think back on it now, how purple and damp I used to get, the fumes, gnashings and spittles I expended! But now as embark I do upon this age old sentimental tour, all, I feels is fondness, forgiveness and longing. o what nostalgia - weeps of it!

- is there in my heart for the *Welsh Theatre of Invisibility* of the fifties, the *Wars of the WACO Word Lords* of the, sixties, the *Theatre of Bad Odours* of the seventies, and wonder of wonders! - Tobyobe's Theatre of Carrots and Footballs of the eighties? o give me that old WACO Leech-Farm time again with all its gags and gagas, gangs and gangsters! 'Ha, ha!' - again to you Supremo Matty *'Three Thousand Acres'* Prichardo, Geoffrey *'Ostrich Egg'* Axleworthy, Councillor *'Jockstrap'* Lewis - 'the Man with the Cleanest Mind in the World,' Ian *'Self-Growing'* Bell, - teacher Grant *'Indignation'* Williams - what a stand was there against public hard ons! - Roger *'Jargoneer'* Tomlinson, Brigadier *'Disgusted'* Watkins, Jimmy *'Green Tree'* Evans, Alan V. Williams - *'the Colossus of the Short-stemmed Pipe',* Clive *'Whirling Dervish'* Barnes of Llandovery – bright Dreadlox of Brixtonia, Andy *'No, thenk you!'* Manley, Bill *'Prince of Egg'* Shakesburt, Jesus *'Ecce Homo'* Christ, and the very Sodom of all our dear Gomorrahs: Swansea Town with the memory of its Matron-Gladiator Strip Riot of '86 still immaculate. Hot ladies of Swansea, the twenty first century and its wankers salutes you still! Now over to the stinking purlieus of the Museum and its widespread unholy rot. Into the vestibule, (watch the creepy-crawlies there!) Over the mold and fungus here to the Books, see, done out in pigskin, like their main contributors. Into *Fond Recollections and Outstanding Utterances* thena willy-nilly dip to begin with.

What have we here? Yes, I see it now! - Margam County Park in '87 and Wales's first real live insect play. Yes, began as a Passion Playas I recall until that plague of... 'locusts' was it? No, *'fleas!'* of course, 'which fell voraciously on the cast, the twelve disciples' and other higher ups, but miraculously the five thousand who'd bought tickets never even got a nibble. Jesus Christ - thank God! And Pontius and his brother Pilate 'were too engaged' to even brush off the little buggers and soldiered right on to the Crucifixion, Ecce Homo! - without a single scratch! Bravo Pontius, bravo Pilate and bravo Jesu boyos!

### *Chuckle and wink, makes you think.*

What next? What's this? Yes, the one gleambeam in all the poison ivy -Jimmy Roose-Evans, Celtic Director, distinguished genius and stipendiary priest to boot, came up with a fresh-smellin' first for Wales - the Festival of the Tree, at the Centre of Caring and the Arts, in courteous Bleddfa Yes, if but for an hour 'the Fir became Attis, the Cedar Osiris, the pine Dionysus, the Myrtle Artemis, and the Apple' -jelly. And in the Vestibule picked out in gold on the *Motto Plaque* (to make it last - how they tried to stamp it out): 'A tree may be motionless but birds come to it.' The 'Stipendiary Priest' speaks with the voice of Revelations, which is quite right. 'And it was commanded them that they should not hurt the grass of the earth, neither any green thing, neither any tree.' Spot on and sod offProminents, Wales still has need of thee, Jimmy *'Green Tree'* Evans! What's the next quote now? How the moss is overgrown between these soggy leaves... yes! *'The Colossus o/the Short-stemmed Pipe',* founder of Wales's most National

198

Laughable Theatre, upon his open-ended 'retirement': 'Put a human being in prison, deprive him of books and music for thirty years and you will produce a sad empty creature with a narrow field of vision.' True, yes, don't you think? Pity, too long for a plaque, but in the top ten for Utterances (without Meaning). 0 Colossus, no dandelions will ever sprout out of your meerschaum mausoleun, all sixty tons of it, raised by unabashed public conscription, still giving off nauseous fumes. No, never I say!

*How I used* **to** *red-up* **at** *his gormless cabbage rows of sentences but now I just chuckle and wink piecemeal! Makes you think!*

Yes, let's have a dekko at the art. What was passing on the stages of Wales at this privateering time? Yes, Moving Being 'was echoing Viennese cafe life with *These Great Times at Le Chateau de Saint Donat,'* while at Le Chateau de Caldicot we had 'a little baroque music in the lavish atmosphere of the Court of Loius XIV, danced by the *Consort de Danse Baroque'.* Vivaldi, boyo, here is one Taff you veritably slayed with your artful arabesques! At Porthcawl' s Grand Pavilion at the same very instant 'unfolded the immortal story of Mario Lanza'. Weep Caruso, for you have noplace yet in the Pavilion with our Prominents! HiJinx followed up a success with their own *Fall of the Roman Empire* - at the Barnsbury Estate Tenants Hall, as well they might, why not? How's that for you Quo bloody Vadis, what about Welsh hiraeth!? But let's look at something more simian... yes! Chapter's artfull Centre, by Canton of Cardiff.

Miraculous. Another charismatic Arts Supremo, Glaswegian Neil Wallace, Crown Prince of Moaners (his words) blow me split for the Gorbals to be charismatic there. Charismatic Yorkshire Man Dave Clark came in with a word about 'brass': 'Nothing happens without dollops,' (did he mean his thirteen thousand dollop salary?) and swore that Chapter was 'no radicalhot-bed now.' In spite of this, nevertheless and notwithstanding it, the very creditable *A Word About Waves* went on. In this piece' a surrealistic man teaches his cat to say "haberdasher" "apothecary" and "Godalming" interspersed with scenes of primeval hunting to this verse: "We once had gills behind our necks when we were very, very small," *and chorus:*

**"Yoghurt yoghurt I dropped, I dropped yoghurt today, yoghurt on my tie, I dropped today. I thought yoghurt, yes, yoghurt".'**

Ye Magic Flutes of Handels and Spinozas, ye too, despair and die!

Chapterfull's first top international ladies: Deborah Levy, Liz Hughes-Jones, Then Nagel Rasmussen and Lora Herrendorf, then waded in with their Magdalena Project, the first bit of which was *You Strike the Woman, You StrikeRock!* Wales's other first top feminist group launched *Pax* 'an allegory of our times with four women who represent Europe and the Past, Future, the Here and

Now and Patriar-chy and Materialism.' Meanwhile Cardiff's *International Festival of Theatre* continued - with a film! *Swimming to Cambodia* followed by 'pop, funk, dub' and Sosta Palmizi's *Il Cortile* there went to, yes! - Sosta Palmizi! Top plaque there. But up the road after golden-dollop 'face-lifts' the Cardiff New became 'the nearest thing to heaven in Wales'. (See charismatic illustration from brochure.) 'The New has changed forever! Come, glide up the graceful new spiral staircase under swooping chandeliers to the fresh glory of the rediscovered auditorium, a true feast, a paradise which has everything you most value in life - style, grace, beauty!' Top Outstandingest Utter Utterance of them all! Bravo New! And what nobler vehicle to launch this Celtic Aladdin's Cave of Tosh but Ack-Ack Ayckboum's A *Chorus of Disapproval* backed by the glittering, unheard of Royal Baccarat Scandal- a feast for out-ofwork indigenes.

*I used to burst outright at such puking, aimless waste, but now with a titter I merely pull the chain and move off with all the idiot vigour of no hope. Still, makes you think, don't it?*

Don't go away, more stuff here. Always gets stuck solid shit on the Sherman Leech-Farm pages... there! What went on? Yes, I see, the usual undiscovered twentieth century masterpieces - the almost neglected *Death of a Salesman,* the partially obscure *Glass Menagerie* by a Williams, Shakesburt Ad Nauseum in Mexico, *King Lear* in Brenin Llyr (another feast for the indigenes) andAck-Ack's not totally un-ignored *Taking Steps.* Then on to take the Top Terrifying Realism Plaque for the' six wall sockets and plugs flown in from the USA' for S.Shepherd's *True West.* Entertaining Mr Sloane - with its row of flaccid penises which would have been better covered'. Then down to bongoes with the Sherman Company on Safari, six solid Welsh actors in Shakesburt yet again. *Midsummer Night's Wet Dream,* playing in Uganda, Botswana, Gabarone, Khartoum -lovers, mechanicals, fairies, all ending in Victoria Falls. White Man's Burden Plaque for *'Ostrich Egg'* Axleworthy! While all the time the otherene Sherman top director Gilly Adams kept nagging playwright-artist- sculptor Alan Osborne, 'Michaelangelo is a subject you have to tackle, and of course – in authentic ensemble!' 0 silly billy Gilly, tell. Why ask? The Michaelangelo Plaque was made for Alan and 'in ensemble' long before your Sistiner ever came along! The Sherman's renowned *Write On Festival* had not a single write off thanks to Gilly and her modem Michaelangelo!

*Chucklee, chucklee, winkee, winkee.*

Then unbelievabubbly, the Sherman Leech Farm positively 'reeled'. It came 'under siege' from Phil 1. Stines of the University Finance Committee who pulled 213,000 dollops 'from right under our feet!' *'Ostrich Egg'* became 'shell shocked' at these 'staggering blows.' Formidable John Morris at once accused tiny Minister Wyn Roberts 'of appalling ignorance of the Sherman' (an ignorance which the whole world shares to this day - to its delight.) Other Sherman Man Co-director, the indisputably talented Mikee James, wrote the profoundly disturbing *Save the Sherman* songee. But the suggestion of a glittering 'Celebrity Reception' won an instant Topwortby Plaque with ostrich crest and coot and sent morality soaring again. But dew-drop dollops soon eased the pain again - from minus 213,000 College dollops to plus 60,000 College dollops to plus 120,000 South Glam dollops to plus 50,000 Sherman Trust dollops to finally Minister Pete Walker's chip-in take-over 875,000 irresistible civic dollops down, with new Leech Farmers in the van paying peppercorns for 125 years - and I'm not the one to break your heart, it was side-splitting! But in this very moment of Top Turf Accountancy, the most fell blow fell. Shining *'Ostrich Egg'* himself was knocked out of the crawling by fuckin; statutory retirement. Big-hearted as ever, he humbly crowed: 'Time to let someone else have a chance.

Other gruesome valedictories made Outstanding Utterances too. 'Theatre is as essential as Parks, like in Germany. ' (Before me) 'the people of Cardiff had been laid waste by TV and had been perfectly happy in the sixties to have no theatre. (After me) all that 'grocery-shop-cash-and-profit-and-loss mentality' was swept away. Yes, *'Ostrich Egg'* had indeed 'built a desert out of a cultural oasis' - for when his monument went up, the trees for miles around shed their leaves and strange rancid brylcream stains appeared on the scalp of Bill Shakesburt, whose head *'Ostrich Egg'* had accepted as his own. Yes, he was at once convinced too 'there was room for another theatre in Cardiff, for large scaley productions. ' His! The old *Prince of Wales* 'I'd love to run it,' he said, 'eyes shining'. And why? 'Because there are lots of things not happening here because there is nowhere for them to happen' - except after him! Appointed, never disappointed (on full salary) is his song and the Greenest Plaque for greed and envy is his own. Most Fulsome Flattery Plaque goes to Jon Holliday *(South Wales Echo)* and Nicole Sochor *(Western Mail)* with lotsa charismatic *'Ostrich Egg'* on their face. 'This engaging, shy, unflamboyant man... the Creator of the Sherman... the Spiritual Father of theatre professionals throughout the world' whose 'infectious enthusiasm casts a glow over all he touches.' The man 'possesses perfect credentials. ' Come on Holliday, remember the 'Ibadan Connection'? Principal Bill *'Kaiser'* Bevan's jobs for the Ibadan yobs? Remember *Rebecca* the 'radical magazine for Wales', and its exposes? (Spring 1978 *'Kaiser Bill'* issue, obtainable through any public library.) Why, Ibadan Axleworthy's post was never even advertised (as required by law). And after Rebecca's 'publish and be damned', strange - no writs flew. And remember the later bankruptcy of University College and the Kaiser's abrupt 'retirement'? Why the works of *'Ostrich Egg'* are full of 'pus and bile and hatred of the world' as he himself admits, 'unproduceabubble!' As for - 'Creator and 'Spiritual father' - chuck it Holliday!

*Such barefaced academic crookery once used to turn me tripes to trots, but it's no more shifty now*

*than running out of toilet paper on the jon. With those bare-faced Ibadanians well in hand, why, I just crease myself, wipe my eyes and then my bum and hum.'*

'Above all things, for you for me, for free, truth beareth away the victoreee!' So like *Rebecca* publish and be - saved!

*Chucklee, chucklee...*

Let's flip over now... yes! Swansea Town's famed and far healthier nut and Taff skullduggeries. Let's see... yes, there's capital the *Grand's* become!-whose 'face-lift' was more golden than Cardiff's New Paradise. 'Dollops answereth all things' as it says, and the Grand had, yes, was it, yes, more than seven million dollops - and I mean just that - from Ewerupp some say. Tho' no one's sure. Sometimes it's four million, or two or two and a half, see, no one knows exactly anymore, here or there, approximately, give or take, the work was finished so late two months at the latest. 'Not we,' whined the sub-contractors. 'Don't look at us,' gulped the theatre sub-commitee, 'it was blind destiny.' 137,000 dollops gone absent if not AWOL. 88,000 already declared missing for the next time round.

*If you asks me, they need more audits than auditoriums.*

*The Charmer of Splot*

So, whatever the scapegoats, in stepped a fresh-faced new District Auditor (like that it really is in Gwalia!) and declared his quiet but intense satisfaction 'with the new steps taken to counter chronic over-spending, inadequacies, inefficiencies and procedures.' Listen now to the sound of squelchy dollops coming down in Swansea Town. The final Grand budget settled at a beggarly 777,890 dollops per delicious anum an' anus! Cheers, and some condemned were pardoned also. Once-collared Paul' *Scapegoat'* Tyson got off the hook, innocent as a daisy after 'two of the most miserable years of my life.' He never done what they said he done, never milked the bar of booze, never touched expenses overnight, nor falsified the odd account or two up to the vast tune offive hundred pounds to the nearest sou. So Paul 'hugged and kissed relatives after the verdict.'

*For meself, Paul, r d have been crapping from their chandeliers and peeing* on *their posh auditoriums*

*like Jesus and his brother Harry! But now* at *one hundred and fifty three, with* a *light-hearted wave*

of *the* *hand I just leave all such protest movements* to *better, younger more charismatic bowels than*

*mine. Good luck, Paul, hammer the sods for every shifty 3,111,560 farthings they habitually get!*

But no more had innocence been declared than further theatre criminality broke out all over again.

*Edward sings*

Another member on the Grand's 'Manager Team', one brave and parfit Huw Knight was 'suspended' but, there's apt, 'only for minor misdemeanours'. Five hundred perhaps again? But still all secret, see. Huw, boy, think you'd better have a word with Paul.

## Winkee...

So willy-nilly for all the rolled gold in the Grand. Funny fiasco followed funny fiasco, see. The theatre's application for a 'pub-type license' was turned down because the police, see, are against more beer in the centre of Swansea. 'New gimmicks make people drink more every day,' they say, 'drinking has reached breaking point.' (Who needs' gimmicks '? - a good Taff will drink a pub dry at the drop of a fly!) But Spokessergeantpersons was adamant-like: 'Every weekend 7,500 drunks spill out of pubs putting a strain on police resources... ' And while battling with these myriad Taffo pissers, 'forty-four smash and grabs took place and vans were overturned amid chaotic scenes.' And meanwhile down at the prison, 'loud-mouthed inmates used foul language ' while 'conducting family feuds over the twenty-five foot high prison wall' - all this in fair Glamorgan Street? So Councillor *'Jockstrap'* Lewis, the 'man with cleanest mind in the world' comes down with a bang and backs calls for 'firm action' against these midnight Capulets. To cool it, lads, Volcano Theatre wanted to perform inside the walls - regularly. Too late, Volcano, for Swansea's moral shock troops poured in headline back-up indignations. 'Head

History Teacher' Mrs Lesley F. Davies reviled *The M erthyr Uprising of* 1831 for 'being littered with foul language, sexual innuendo and unfortunate references to the teaching profession.' Councillor *'Jockstrap'* rallied his Indignants, demanding the expulsion of all gay students and lecturers from the centre of Swansea and urged the removal of all condoms tossed about by the students during *Aids Awareness Week. 'Jockstrap'* went on to recoil from 'the rather explicit wording of the (Aids) brochure' which thing 'encouraged promiscuity' and was delighted when lecturer-director Paul Heritage's *Principal Parts* were cut off. 'No funds for fairies' was the watchword from Swansea's super-talced self-elected Squire Scrubbing Brush. Super *'Jockstrap'!* But curse St David for the Taffo-deriders and delinquents who 'jostled, abused and spat on' *'Jockstrap'* as he escaped to his lovely little toyshop *Kattoys.* Standing be- tween two sixteen stone 'rugby-playing-type' minders, he announced he'd stand as Tory for Swansea east in the next erection even if it was his last.

*But I Jockstrap' - Taffo still you are - chuckle, chuckle - don't you realize that a damaged halibut at the bottom of the barrel smells sweeter far than all of the English upper crusties stuck together?*

*WAC'O chap celebratin' the end of a Dedwydd Jones play*

*'Jockstrap's p*laque's up there see, the only one without a drop of bat-shit on it. Never knew those little black-winged harbingers of evil could be so delicate, makes Dracula almost prissy, steering clear of *'Jockstrap'*. And you should see his monument, a spotless fifty-foot high cricket 'box'! About the only thing you can say for *'Jockstrap'* and his High Indignancies is at least they fulfill the provisions of the Clean Air Act - but only in a vacuum on a Funny Farm. But sad at Swansea, after every note of virtuous hope, dammo, comes near bluddy moral collapse! This time it was Berkoff's *Greek* which created Wales-wide upset with its 'lust, ambition and soap(!) Berkoff's Hellenic filth was followed by *Fur Coat andNo Nickers-I* ask you! -with its 'rank duchesses, tipsy vicars, four-letter postmen and devil-may-care grandads.' Is there no health in us? Yes! Sir Wholesome-Benefit suddenly came in with Mark's and Spencer's *Airs and Promata' s Dance and Cello Interpretation of Eduard Munch's Paintings* (A.P.D.C.I.E.M.P.) - howzzat!? And a late spate of at least 100 clean (more or less) events with 180 Companies or was it vice versa? Or was the numbers right at all? Anyway there was *The Common Fun of Earth* which at once restored pleasing appearences, while the *Theatre of Sculpture* was most moving. On went *The Man and Antonin Artaud* too and the women next, Sylvia Pankhurst, Mrs Beeton, Lizzie Siddel, the Pre-Raphaelite's Artist's Model at least. The *Poor Girl* was produced but 'in mist-shrouded rags' and sadly *A Deadly Nightcap* turned into a 'yawn evening' in spite of its spate of TV stars. (See the The Most Boring Plaque up there, sends you to sleep, don't it?) But after all this theatrical Alpine soap, our hopes was bashed again.

Spiritual ruin stared Swansea in the lower tum-tum with TV's Kathy Staff in *See How They Run* who made her 'rumpled leg-wear' (sagging stockings - gettit?) downright overpoweringly sexy - as if Swansea's members needed any more excitation. Ecce Homo, they'd get sexed up over a cucumber close to a curtain ring. However, classical values were somewhat revived a bit with Bill Shakesburtee's *Timon of Athens* set in feudal Japanese (Farewell 0 Hero Heato!) done to a turn by The Rat Company. The cultural balance was finally tipped – somewhere - byTopical Theatre with its *Desperate Men.* Still more events rolled on. The Fringe Festival with 'over 300 performances' from Pontardawe to charismatic Port Talbot. First thing, two thousand five hundred and seventy four one man and one woman shows called *Dylan and Caitlin* were reported on the starboard bow but General Boredom sank the lot. However Dylanmania did win out, the wretch. The very tablecloth from the very Italian New York restaurant upon which the very bard-boyo drunk, drooled, dribbled, doodled and dined was on display for spaghetti lovers allover Tiger Bay at the DT Bookshop in Swansea itself, while just up the road 'a veritable orgy of Who's Who in the Welsh Theatre' re-re-re- recorded *Under Milk Pudding* from which the play emerged with udders flying. Most Bulging Udder Plaque for 'Who's Who'.

### Wink, wink...

Meanwhile, the Festival's Organiser and Word Person Robbie Moffat stuck to the point: 'The Fringe is a key... a powerful magnet... which has a knock-on effect...

towards a national platform and... stops the best from de-camping. ' But 'the politics of the theatre are desperately worrying at the moment. The WACO is not fighting in its comer and experimental investigative theatre is getting side-lined.' Much more than a mere Plaque -let there be knighthoods for such eloquencies! But plough on the Festival did in spite of 'cock ups, late starts, double bookings wrong venues, shameless pull outs' and one show *'Careless Talk'* may have got lost altogether.' Press on Robbie tho' Swansea Town's 4,750 dollop contribution didn't cut much cackle and West Glam's weighty 600, all in pounds, left the next festival 'in some doubt.' Swing from the chandeliers Robbie, boyo, forget the vomit bag I'd let it all hang out!

*More dollops for Robbie I say! Don't the Prominents yet know that it is Swansea's glorious loons and not the Grand's spitoons that will make the world safe for Welsh democracy one day?*

Into this welter of contemporary drama now fell the most unwelcome death of all, towering Emlyn Williams's. 'A great loss to Wales and the world', wept Minister Pete Walker and sang:

*choke for me,*

*choke for you,*

*choke for all –*

*In Tory blue'.*

Top Crocodile Chokes and a First in Incoherent Grief! Pete, the Plaque shines through your tears as Latimer lauds its Great!

***Piss* on *you*, *piss* on *me*, *'av* a *nice cuppa tea,it comes* to *us all. Sorry, just testing.***

And Tobyobe puts on *Night Must Fall,* prophetic vision of departed Emlyn in the Emlyn Williams Studio. Fitting for an indigene to have a little room. The Saxon-Condescension Plaque is Tobyobe's all. But back to Swansea for a last honest, human if not native, touch. One Grand Welsh Husband - age and condition yet unknown - leapt up in *West Side Story* during that most tender duet *Tonight* and yelled, 'my wife should be singing that song!' 'Dragged' he was 'to the bar. Lights were smashed in a violent struggle. Police were called.' But this valiant Swansea consort was later released 'due to lack of genius.' This sweet incident gave rise to the well-known West Glam saying, 'A Welsh husband always stands up for his wife, even in the Grand.' I'd like to have known the husband's name - and had a look at his missus too. This was the husband of Swansea's most striking hour and it still is most thumbed in the *Book of Fond Recollections.* And now go West to the Torch of Milford where new young man, Ian Bell out of Angleterre, was simply revelling in originality. Celebrating the theatre's tenth anniversary on earth with Ack *Ack'sRelatively Speaking-which* was the very first piece 'that pushed the boat out' one decade before, 'now come full circle,' but with one overwhelming difference

- 'the new sets are vastly superior... they now have self-growing grass.' Later Ian *'Self-Growing'* Bell launched a 'vitamin C' *Dr Faustus.* For Ian knew that Dr Faustus 'had huge bits by dross-hackwriters in it.' Ian sensibly 're-drafted' the play 'to retain the gold Marlowe wrote.' And everybody felt better after that, didn't we? Then *'Self-Growing'* called in the astonishingly former Supremo Brigadier *'Disgusted'* Watkins out of Cheltenham to put on Sir Peter Hall's *Animal Farm* to galvanize a pigeon - which it did not do. 'Even as a 'panto' it proved a bore.' So bless the Friends of the Torch 'who had donated hand-rails for the auditorium,' for these now assisted the charismatic sleep-walkers out to safety. Then, after the *'Disgusteds'* and *'Animals'* and *'Halls'* and *'Ack-Acks'* and *'Vitamins',* a slice of Welsh strife-torn life was on, *Little Yankee* set in '32, about the right of Milford fisherfolk to have 'the dog-fishes and damaged halibuts at the bottom of the net.' Quipped Master Bell: 'In the early days we'd do a *Dracula* or a *Werewolf,* now we're doing a Richard Crane's *Crippen.'* Top Oblique Utterance for Bell. Then the crises mUltiplied like cowpats till they culminated in a Top Dollop Plaque for the Torch, a most enviable distinction, for this: 'If you are getting five hundred thousand dollops and you lose ten thousand dollops, the impact is not nearly so great as if you were getting one hundred thousand dollops and you lose ten thousand dollops. ' Well-dollopped sir! It's swipes like that that make the Torch the 'cultural focus' that it is! Ta you, boyo Bell.


*Still, makes you wink.*

And Dollops took all as well at Tobeyobe's Leech Farm up in noble Mold. Testy Tobyobe, crazed by desire for eminence, utters and recollects so outstandingly that a whole new wing would not house his myriad plaques and gems. With something like over one million dollops 'to play around with', Tobyobe actually done a few sly little 'overspends' like up-grading chum-posts twice which put him in the moldy to over 50,000 dollops.

*A mere piddle in thy pants I say, why all the fuss?*

But nasty NALGO demanded a major investigation into the finances of the theatre.' Tobyobe riposted by blaming NALGO for 'not consulting him' and launched his Festival '88 to recoup the silly losses. 'I'll put my shirt on this Festival,' he panted. 'Wales has had need of something like this for a long time'. Which pearl looks perfect carved into his fifty-four foot square crystal headstone with its perpetual wreaths of hairy bittercress and common scurvy grass. Yes, the word 'Wales' is constantly on Tobyobe's lips - and nowhere else.

*Chuckle, chuckle for* a *moment now with me* as *I salute the memory* of *these unassuming titans* of

*our past - in spite* of *their putrefying remains. Hang on. Just buttoning up. There. Ta.*

Yes, back to Wales and Tobyobe. A swift and penetrating journalist, one David Adams, analysed Tobyobe's audiences and found: They are mainly English, elderly and well-heeled. The most regular

217

theatre-goers being between 56 and 64... and the majority of occasional patrons between 65 and 74.' Ecce Homo, a geriatric home for withered Tories deep in the crackle and sweep, cottage-burning territory! Cymru am buggered, Tobyobe wins the biggest Saxon Plaque of the century. So off went his 'Welsh' Festival '88, hardly surprisingly with *Arms and the Man* and *An Inspector Calls,* with the usual hordes of TV /West End stars to ride to glory on. Then *Paris Match* by the Parisian who gave Denbigh *Le Cage aux Foiles.* Then whammo! – on with Bristol's 1950 hit, the charismatic Ruritanian Romance, *Captain Carvailo.* Into overdrive with Tobyobe's *McBurt* with the three witches 'depicted as a boy in leg calipers, a girl in a see-through dress', and Seyton 'brought on sooner than expected'.

Then into the scoop of a sludge":gobbling ego, a four-hundred year old play, *Edward II/,* about 'English jingoism and sordid love,' attributed to Bill Shakesburt. (Bill's *Edward /* and *II* had been 'far too dire.') But Tobyobe dropped the 'attr Shakesburt' because Shakesburt really *did* write Tobyobe' s *Edward II/* 'then went away to digest how to write plays and came back with *The Comedy of Errors'* -so there! Tobyobe frequently congratulated himself on his 'archeologists's role.' 'We should swan in as well, rather than leaving it all to the RSC.' It was lovely because 'to direct in a proven mould is to direct in a strait-jacket' and it was fine because Edward III was 'a Renaissance Man' (200 years before the Renaissance?). 'Talk till you're blue in the face,' Tobyobe bellowed, 'we're treading on virgin ground!' A virile utterance, still on some of our faded sweat-shirts in the Museum bins. Onward

Tobyobe'swanned' with *Queen and Country* - Welshmen fighting for their Queen, why not? - but Queen Anne this time. 'The whole putrid pile of irrelevance' as Shakesburt put it, topped with old, old Etonian Humphrey Trumpeter of Lyttleton. Yes, no bombings or burnings blur Tobyobe' s worn-out antique Home Counties tunnel vision. But Tobyobe's right-hand mouth-piece one B.Thackry, dutifully set up, replied: 'Many theatres in Wales are now refusing to take our touring productions' (such as *Getting Out)* because of 'scheduling problems' or they simpabubbly say, 'We're too small.' Then Thackry pounded on like a Marcher Lord, 'We are important for Wales!' Implacable Plaque-Trap for Thackry - see it up there solid as Norman shite! And old Tobyobe went offfor sherry with the White Settlers of Denbigh with ne'er a single complementary for the overworked fire-chiefs of Gwynedd. Listen:

*"They've made pretence into a science:*

*Card-sharpers of the art committees*

*Working all the provincial cities,*

*They cry 'Eccentric' if they hear*

*A voice that seems at all sincere.*

*Fold up their table and their gear*

*And with the money disappear."*

('Epitaph for the Subsidised Theatre' from *The Prelude* by Patrick Kavanagh. Spot on, Pat.)

*A little girl gazes at a gull*

Now look across yonder in the murkiest, Most mongoloidishest corner of the Night Soil. There, that's where it started swelling. The *Welsh Arts Council Monument* I mean. Appalling isn't it? At first the site was as discreet and sealed in as a missile silo and about as creative. With a hedge of deadly nightshade around it to give it a bit of life. Over the century though we found that the herds of local pigs and cattle felt this strange inexplicable urge to defecate on the spot. Nothing would discourage them. The bulls were especially copious. Well, as you can see, these irresistible animals have raised a *Gigantic Tower o/Veritable Dung* (G.T.V.D.) over sacred WACO and its undeniable Prominents within. It's a favourite with the tourists but only from upwind. Careful, masks are provided if you want to approach. Yes, the *Highest Brown Arts Tower in the World,* no Plaque is foul enough for it, and we like to play this little tape as your eye rests fondly on the mammoth shittyscape. Listen then to Roger *'The Dodger'* Tomlinson, the WACO's top ancient *Jargoneer,* a prize among men and eloquent beyond all normal ken: 'The overall drama budget has increased from 1.7 million dollops to 1.8 million and from 7.5 million to 8.5 million in very real terms. We have only 1,827,700 to play with against a total of 2,402,607 million demanded.' Listen, humanity of Wales, indeed for all of time, especially at the back, listen! 'Cashcrippled we stand aghast with gloomy forecasts of a wholesale arts collapse which will be at the watershed, major chunks are tapered off - stark illustrations of real retrenchment in spite of our strong-worded dismay. We cannot keep dear WACO's head above water because of these down-turns, due only to dear WACO's own inescapable committments. The twin cornerstones of WACO have proved barren ground for sponsors. All art will wither and die in a survival of the fittest scenario. Unless we roll up our sleeves to assess the quality oflife, all art will continue to be hard-pressed. I have done all I can to throw up ring fences round experimental companies.' Ecce homo! - The Green and Yellow Matter Plaque. Moreover, Roger took Plaque, Album and Book with 'creative hibernation' for 'out of work' and 'cyclical funding only' for 'sod off!' See thel *argoneer'* s banner at the entrance fluttering brokenly in the wind as its winner always did.

But to dastards now, for Roger *largoneer* got bounced right out of the WACO swamp. His three-year contract was not renewed so Roger could resign 'open-endedly' like *Colossus* and *the Egg* 'because he felt he could be more effective outside.' (Why stay six years inside then?) But tho' outside like 'links would be maintained on a consultancy basis.' So farwell *'Dodger'* as you enter charismatic 'Research Services into Customer Care and Arts Management.' We'll watch your space with pleasure.

**But what really happened? Were the cubicles all engaged? Were all the outlets blocked. Or did they simply run out of toilet paper? Chuckle, chuckle, wipe, wipe, I'm afraid we shall never know. Thank**

**Ecce Homo**.

Nevertheless Supremo Matty *'Three Thousand Acres'* Prichardo got 're-elected' again for three years all right, to soldier on with Tom-Tom Owen WACO Chairman to further enrich the language of Shakesburt. But with God's greatest gift to the cliche gone, words will never be as indistinct again.

Prichardo tried with 'These are exciting times for the arts, never has there beeen so much talent... I shall explore every avenue... time is of the essence.' Not bad I suppose, but lacks the *'Dodger's* sparkle, don't you think? And Prichardo's vision of the new WACO was not quite as incredible as the great *Jargoneer's.* 'WACO will be much more business oriented... it will be necessary to seek resources instead of doling out taxpayer's money.' He visualised 'credit card schemes and sponsored stamps and extra penny projects and arts lotteries. ' However the arts lottery went down the drain before it even got off the ground. It cost the WACO 5,000 dollops simply to be told by McCann and Mathews that such lotteries were illegal in the first place under the Lotteries and Amusements Act. Ferocious Hard Business Plaque there, Prichardo! But again five thou's just a piddle in his pants as well. As Prichardo said, see: 'Wales seems to have come to terms with being a poor country,' then turned his mind to more mellow dramas. Prichardo wondered about 'the stop-go nature of drama... where much-acclaimed playwrights flare into brilliant life for a moment, then - silence! Why?' The 'I Wonder Why' Plaque for Prichardo was shared by B Thackray (double me up those two) but the Bonanza Hypocrisy Plaque was all Prichardo's own. Bursaries to writers (suspended since 1984) were abruptly restored in '88 giving Prichardo 'much pleasure'. Little wonder, for during the entire period of this ban, Prichardo had been enjoying the enormous royalties of - yes! a writer! and a play writer to boot - Aga Christie's *The Mousetrap.* And not only this but Prichardo was also Chainnan of Booker McConnell Publishers (Authors Division) with some say in the handing out of the 'prestigious'Booker McConnel Prize - to writers! All this 'Give me!' and 'I take!' Welsh writers didn't get a sou. Unastonishing? Ratherish! And, to add a little prick to the salt, Prichardo plans an Aga Christie

Festival on three thousand acres a year, for 1990. And who's going to pay for that little lot?

*Wink, wink, I wonder why?*

And when I look down now on Supremo Prichardo's streaked, sinking monument here (young he went, all of 103) funny, all I can see is a very small mouse in a very small trap.

*Arse, cock, come, cunt, fart, ball{s}, fuck, piss, shit, quim, shag, twat, wank, turd - don't forget with a Prichardo you can chuckle all the way to the grave!*

And writer John Onnond assisted by Vanena Webb again renewed that antique call for 'an open, demQcratic and independent WACO with no secrecy, no closed sessions, no confidential minutes, no secret decisions, no last minute announcements'. A WACO for Magna Carta's sake, from which there is 'aright of appeal., No answer necessary from a body some of whose key members have voted themselves in for life. But listen:

*They're not pheasant pluckers,*

*They're the pheasant plucker's mates,*

*They're only plucking pheasants because*

*The pheasant plucker's late.*

Etonia and Oxfordia Prichardo went on to endorse Tobyobe's Anglia philosophy of Wales, 'An established audience for drama has not yet emerged in Wales.' Yet tranquil and far-sighted David Adams insists: 'there is actually a whole body of evidence to show that people in Wales are prepared to see work they know nothing about' citing the very fact that 'having no fixed theatre tradition' urges people to try new plays. Certainly productions like Cordell's *Rape of the FairCountlyand* Chatwin's *On the Black Hill* (neither by Welshmen but all about Wales) played to capacity houses. Unknown works and companies also had considerable success with purely Welsh subjects like Theatre 1010 Morgannwg, and 'experimental' Theatre Taliesin of Grangetown with its inter-cultural, tri-lingual (Indian-English- Welsh) production of *Twn Sion Catti,* Moving Being's *Mabinogion,* and the work of Brif Cof. Yet, as pointed out by David Adams: 'the commissioning rate of the main houses in '88 and '89 was: The Torch 2, Theatre Clwyd 1, Sherman Theatre 0.'

As Mr Adams observes so unmyopically: 'Good work is unlikely to get a production in ally main Welsh house.' Conceived in a wilderness, born in a bog, raised in a desert these 'main houses' finally died in a swamp. Please witness the blank corruption all around you. Now to the black lists of the Prominents' stamped-on, shat on, coffee-stained, script chuck-outs - the right stuff telling 'the stinking truth'. I see lots of it still endures here and there, never horrible, ever beautiful, doing the old modest rounds. Like Keith Baxter's *Barnaby and the Old Boys,* Duncan Bush's *Sailing to America* and especially the permanently smashing *House of America* by Ed Thomas.

*Millions* **of** *daffodills* **on** *yer, Ed.*


Even D. Jones's weird and renegade *Saxon* still buzzes around, plus his 'Book of Scraps' as he calls his devlish chuckles and glees, the *Black, Book on the Welsh Theatre* - and *Saxon* first produced... let me see, all of ninety years ago... next to the drowned Cartref near Cardigan. Brought to bear by the skilled and crystal insights of Colin Powell King of Theatre Annwn itself. Annwn still salutes its children, Colin Powell more than King! Where's my notes, yes, what was said about writers now? Yes, got it. Mr Chris Ryde of Equity: 'The BBC and HTV are not producing enough material based in Wales, they are not using their indigenous artists.' Always so. Graham Allen, Welsh Writers' Union for 1987: 'Why has the BBC or HTV not offered a single programme connected with the Arts?' 'None' is not yet enough! And the blessed English-writing question? Adrian Mourby, Head of Radio Drama: 'There seem to be more outlets for playwrights writing in Welsh than in English.' Kevin Thomas, Welsh Union of Writers: 'Let's have more English-language Welsh drama. The writers of Wales are ready. ' For dammo ever and a day! Director Gilbert Lloyd Roberts: 'Wales must be the only country in the world where TV arrived before theatre' - with dollops and chances galore down the plughole, right, Gilbert, boyo? What's this? Yes, letter of total resignation from Wales. Carl Tighe, dramatist, goes ex -pat in '87. Listen: 'After twenty years I have decided to cease all connection with Welsh Theatre: 'the Swansea Grand, the Sherman, the Sherman Arena, Mold, the Torch, Action Pie, Brif Cof, Made in Wales, Hi-Jinx,

Gwent TIE, Masquerade, Backdoor, Spectacle, Chwarae Teg,' (among others) for 'incompetence, indifference, complacency, lack of imagination, missed opportunities, sluggardliness, bad faith, opportunism, personal ambition and greed.' Carl's longest rejection? Nine years. Mold takes this Plaque. Most ugly rejection? Made in Wales made it with 'Nationalist nonsense, peculiar, Irish, threadbare, turgid Polish shit.' Biggest Ignoramus Plaque, again to Made in Wales for rejecting *Uncle Vanya* 'in a Welsh setting with names changed,' as 'too confused in plot with too many characters.' Carl's *Whisper in the Wind* got the muddy boot as well in '87 and promptly went on to win an all-London theatre writing prize in '88. Most terse rejection of the decade: 'A Dedwydd Jones play? No thank you!' from Andrew *'No thank you'* Manley.

**Like Carl, puce as an *aubergine I used* to *get, but* look at *me now - cool* as an *egg!***

But here's a laff to raise your spirit, Carl. In the WACO toilet on my last way out, I heard a Wacomite splutter over his chopper: 'Piss on these smelly scribblers! No amount of deliberate, official neglect, shortsightedness, and insult seems to ever get rid of them!' One hundred and fifty three years, Carl, tells me them WACO's is just one long dirty hoot. And they're right! Nothing ever *can* get rid of us!

And then the Most Undiplomatic Mission since Hiroshima. A 'Working Party' was assembled 'to gather information about new theatre writing in Wales' chaired by one subtle Master Julian Mitchell a downright *English* dramatist. Julian greeted me in his letter with, 'Dear Colleague'!

**Makes you think...**

Anglia Plaque First Class for Julian! Cheers!

**Can't stop peeing over this one.**

And Prichardo, please drop 'Welsh' from 'WACO', please.

One grain of hope, however, after centuries and all those dollops under bridges and all those perks and fees and pees and pilferings and droppings. One body went and finally got it right! A V ANA BAKERIES of Cardiff offered all members of the Welsh Union of Writers 'ten per cent off its cakes and buns' with moreover 'special discounts for weddings.' So, fabulously, it took a rum bun bakery to recognize at last that writers have to eat and that writers too have families to marry up. Golden Plaque to Avana Bakeries with a medal inscribed *'Hero of The Writers of Wales'* with the motto, 'Avana feeds the body, the writers feed the soul.' As dramatist Ed Thomas puts it: 'If there is going to be a revival in Welsh Theatre, we've got to find new forms, new styles, and it must be authentic, original and true to its convictions. If we believe in our Welshness, we've got to express it.' And in his *House of America* and in the Bakeries of

Avana, far from the malodorous pastures of the Swamp and its Brown Towers, far from the squalid and irrelevant Album and Book, is the real Cymru to be found.


### Afternote

*I did indeed present. this tour, with annotations and asides, to the Anarchist Society of the New European Confederation, and ahead of deadline too. The cheeky sods rejected it.*

*'Why?' I asked, 'it is the truth.'*

*'It is not,' they replied.*

*'Truth is but a salute to the natural order and*

*beauty of things,' I said 'if that's What's worrying*

*you.'*

*'It's anarchy we're after" they insisted, 'very much like the subjects of your discourse. If you'd kept your mouth shut and let them have their way anarchy would have won the day for years and years to come! Sorry.'*

*After one hundred and fifty years of rejections, my chuckle could be heard in Mandalay. Later, as I was having my luncheon cup of Chinese Imperial tea at the pensioners' riverside cafe, I was approached by a bearded figure in a 1914 army greatcoat. 'Let me have the discourse,' he begged most agreeably, though he really had very few teeth, 'Anyone with a chuckle that loud deserves to get everything published in two months.'*

'*I* see *you remember,*' I observed with a *grin,* 'that "*above al/ things, truth beareth away the victory*". '

'*Ecce Homo, the charismatic Apocryphal*' he *shouted in delight.* '*Esdras, chapter* 1*, verse* 21!'

So we *shook hands on it and got drunk.*

NOT QUITE THE END

QUIZ:

Please answer the following questions before you read on:

1. What were they up to in Swansea's sand dunes?

2. How high was the 'swear count' of the youth who performed 'Shittin' in a Carrier Bag?'

3. Who could not have sexual intercourse until he had completed The Times crossword?

4. Who poured 'sinister liquids' on 'Scenes from Pembrokeshire'?

5. Why, O why, did 'Golden Boy' leave WACO?

Tho' puzzling questions, these are not beyond all conjecture. They have been tackled by the Charmer of Splott himself, with classic comporteement, elegance, suavity, affability and top manners from all over the world. They did not get past his mordant wit and penetrating insight.

How about you? Read on - if you dare.

# BLACK BOOK ON THE WELSH THEATRE, VOLUME V

**(1990-1991)**

## *'The Charmer of Splott'*

*Welsh Arts Council of Governors with two Courtiers*

*(Enter the CHARMER of Splott, report in hand, smiling excruciatingly. A broad Welsh accent.)*

Evenin' there. Now I'm the bloke from the Charm School of Splott, and I been invited special here tonight to make this foul report here smellin' more sweet. 'Bout public drama it is and the funny goin's on inside like. Just got to lavender it up a bit, fair's fair. What's happened it says, I think, is that recently in Wales there's been a great golden wave of vice, lots of lovely evil abroad, stunnin' turpitudes, over-the-top sin, a very table fall out of pure filth, plus bizarre bugs, odd spoors,

233

ic infections and fey bacilli. That's what it says. I
make it so you smells only roses all the way. We
ers of Splot, we got our sweet mysterious ways,
you'll see.


**See how I'm butterin' you all up already,
smoothin' over all the quiverin' bushes of lust in
here. 'What a charmin' bugger,' you are all thinkin',
aren't you? – sod his vice – am I right? Smile, O
teeth! That's it, there's lovable you lot are – like me.
And no B.O. in the front row either. Yes, I can niff
my audience tonight is more rhan a little devoted to
their tub – bravo! Makes a nice change. Ta. Yes,
refinement of body is a leadin' canon of our Academy
of Charm, tho' I do admit I did see one or two far
from immaculate collars at Chapel last Sunday, but
never mind – wear a scarf!**


Well now, let's open the report. What have we here?
Oh yes, that firebrand Churchman, Dewi Davis, 84,
swore Llanelli had become the New Sodom due to
moral decline and Ma Thatch's Shylock Yuppeeism but
between us I still think Swansea's takes a lot of beatin'.
Cardiff's just a copy cat, Llanelli's nowhere. Up the
Swans I say!

Didn't Splot' s notable hack note, "Modern Swansea
man's chat-ups about as charmin' as a pair of unwashed
football socks." But if modern Swansea man wants to
*come* to our Young Male Laundry Seminars, they'd soon
be as scented as that Owen Boyo foundin' his Tudor

dynasty with a Queen. Bouncy, bouncy, never so clean! Up to him, up to you.

**But for now, chuckle along with me, sin's got its charmin' side, you'll see. Note my comport-ee-ment when I come in, did you? I did not conduct my demeanour with lifted chin, did I? Up to him, up to you. It was only the encitin' smile of Splott you seen. Behold my regard now bewitchin' you all. It is the regard, is it not, of a shy but a mightily appealin' man. Dammo, how the ladies fall for that. Stick with Splott, lads, and I will reveal to you how a man can win golden opinions of hisself despite all the wind and piss from outside.**

Yes, our well-groomed graduates stalk the powers of corridor everywhere. Them Welsh Arts Council sullen boors should've come to me at birth. Converted one golden boy I did, but the rest... them W ACOs is beyond all endearments fair. None of them will ever come on with that allurin' grin of savoir faire like me.

What I'm leadin' up to is that there's been this outbreak of nasty pederasty again in the sand dunes near the 75 million pound Marina opposite the Conservative Club when two courtin' homos, 40, well built, dark hair, pulled their pants up when schoolgirl Miss C. Goodbeer surprised them. Well, Swansea Councillor ' Jockstrap' Lewis, The Man with the Cleanest Mind in the World, Splot' s own former Excelsior of Hygiene, swore, "It is despicable. This foreshore has been a haunt of this type of people for far too long. Such people cause discomfort to people who jog, and make it unattractive to home buyers." Then he urged more police action or take away the dunes! Hear how I said that? Suave like. Like Swansea pansies was tops. Why I'm not boss of The Academy's Suave Gestures Department for nothin'! So chuckle along with me. And grin. Why, Jockstrap's is near perfection even in the grip of sheer masturbation!

After this genial thrust Jockstrap was then threatened on the phone by deep-voiced neo fascists. Heavy breathin' neo-arsonists more like - and then by that dire extremist publication *Class War Cry* with its headline THE BEAST MUST DIE!. But Jockstrap curbed his moral indignation for he knew *War Cry* "had no assets worth sueing." Managed at last I did too, to smooth down *The Chippendales,* the man Yank Strip Show. This time, as the Sex Inspector, said "there was no mob hysteria and the usual display of randy voyeurism that last time made reactions on some soccer terraces look like child's play" referin' to Swansea's Matron Sex Riot of' 88 when they leapt on stage, snatched at loin cloths and rubbed oil all over those luscious boyo botties. Splot's Charmer here saved their nuts this time but I have to say them swingin' *Chippendales* was very gratifyin '.

And still weirder like, rotten little spoors was droppin' here and there in dear Gwalia, creatin' mini scandals like the play *Alice* where the randy White Rabbit would have had Lewis Carrol spinning in his grave at the speed of sound. Then a libidinous germ fell on *Lulu* in far flung Builth. Minister Rearden, a satrap of Jockstrap, enunciated with Splott's now famous crooked grin, "No backwater theatre should show *Lulu* for *Lulu* could stimulate young people and there could be problems." 0 Minister' Lulu' Rearden, spot on ye Splott Alumnus. You showed the world that our charm is available even in cassock form! And too late for us in Theatre Powys a girl in *Tarzanne* had man actors as apes "walkin' with their knuckles trailin' on the ground." Why, one hour at our School would have transformed those simians with spit into Ambassadors with cummerbunds! Next time perhaps. Then the action moved "from the Victorian austerity of the African jungle to the unbridled heat of Gwent" –

**see how I'm slidin' down the bannisters of your libido without you even noticin'. Let me ask you – how did Councillor 'Jockstrap', Minister 'Lulu,' and Dewi 'Soddm' Davies 84, learn just how to how to expel both the skin and seeds of the grape with such decorum, I mean, concealing ejectment the while! How? Your bold dazzler right here. Dammo, he knows his bon ton through and through.**

Then a bit of tainted poetry by Roger' Anarchy' McGough, went and infected every class at Croesyceilog Comprehensive. Listen to this piece of disorderly ordure: "The teacher picked up a boy who was shouting and throttled him then and there, then garotted the girl behind, the one with the grotty hair." What devilish incantation! What moral contagion! But our tasteful trio got them low words banned~ Yet one degenerate eleven-year-old hadthe gall to cry, "The poem was funny. We didn't take it as seriously as Mum." I agree with The Dirt Abolitionists - such poets and ratlets should be thrown instantly into the creepy crawly Royal Palace in Mon-mam-Cymru, a tourist den crawlin' with scorpions and tarantulas! But lookin' on the 'funny side of sin, see, 78,000 visitors came away from the Butterfly Centre near by, with eyelids flutterin' in a very pleasin' way. Ask how at Splott.

Then blowsy old Cardiff got a touch of its own home grown squiggly-wiggly buboes when at the College of Music, a girl dramatist student "squeezed her brightly painted breasts showin' two faces which mimed 'Joy' on the left and 'Despair' on the right." Butto follow, a most base youth "with a very high swear count", went and done *Shittin' in a Carrier Bag,* Low down Swansea trick that is, copycats, what a falling off was there. Dammo, Splot would've teached him to adjust his dress before leaving like any demure gentleman of Tatler and the Swansea Uplands cottages.

Then Wycherly's *CountlY Wife* slipped on behind our backs still "with veiled chunks of bawdiness in." Why does Swansea always stoop so low below the waist for its effects? Must be that plague of foreskins on the beach again. So what Splott sly-like introduced to discourage this in Cardiff was 'saucy opera' at the Tarazzo Restaurant with real life opera stars like, who soon shouted "Bolognese!" to boring pizzas. Your charm leader here's verdict on the course: "the Verdi was particularly well done!" Then the Man Acts chipped in with *The Acts of Man,* to explore people touching people, with penetration disguised under a red bandana. Ole! That's OK! But dammo, underhand again! *The Tart and the Vicar's Wife* stirred the evil slime and rode into the West End with vile panache.

**But let me coach you. When this happens just wave it all through with a silkin' gesture of a pale, well-manicured hand, even as I do now. Never let the sickenin' fishheads see you give a bugger. Indeed!.**

Again we couldn't quite cover up *Hitler's Women* in time - dear Unity and schones Eva – it bein' the one hundredth anniversary of Adolf's demented life-style. But we managed to play it down with Dario Fo's *Facets of Evil* which moved "from a positive excess of vulgarity" to "a simply hilarious look at the Creation," all under our exquisite persuasion, and all was gravitas again.

Yes, Dario, boyo, one hour in Splott's Vestibule of Delight would have banished your eager fever and your tufted palms.

Then would-be naughty Neath took the Swans on for the Vice Championship. Lord Screamin' Sutch promised if he was elected to transform the town "into a Disney-style loony land." But my Lord, if I may interject like, no such change needed. Swansea's streets ahead anyway.

Then the Diplomatic Corps, Theatre Powys, declared a most cultured *Amnesty-without Embarassment* for its wig and skirt snatchers. To celebrate the return of same put on a Victorian Festival with a Caribbean theme and, for safety's sake, for once left out the singed fire-eaters and brought on instead the entire English Philharmonic Orchestra. Yes, heavenly cantos go well with nicked wig and knickers.

Then Swansea done a shameful jape, a phony scare hoax, and "dumped non-existent nuclear waste" on them bum-bare dunes, which I can tell you "caused concern" all round. Indeed put the wind up an entire city but let me add "the bad taste was slammed" by vicars and their curates everywhere, and off the jokesters slunk pursued by virtue to the end.

***Yes, we at Splott, not only charm offal off the walls, we wipe nuclear waste off bare-bum dunes!***

Then this puzzlin' need for apes arose in Swansea's own Plantasia, where *Born in the Gardens* got done. A piece based on "the grunts and facial grimaces of a famous gorilla in Bristol Zoo known as Alfred, renamed Maud in the play, who chattered on and on to a soundless TV and waged war on imaginary termites." After which "a sunburnt porker called Glenda" got a trot-on part in *The Toad,* and in a family type *Gypsy Rose Lee* you could see Polly the Parrot, Holly the Dog and a new-born lamb with no name. Aaaaah! - you go. A lamby-wamby-baa baa. Lovely ! Yes, chuckle along with me.

**You know where Lassie really did come home to from? Well, let me reveal the secret for the very first time. It was home Lassie – to Splott! Yes, do you not remember when Lassie herself winked at us, like that – where'd you think she got that most fetchin' twitch from? Yes, little old distinguee me. Yes, after the**

**moral furnace of Wales, a man's brain should be as
fine as his cuticles, look at mine - like lamb's milk in
te pail. Ha, cute devil I am!**

Then a bit of the round-the-twist politics hit the fan
with arson mugs with "Light a Cottage for Wales" wrote
on. But the Welsh Nationalist Party with its 'no fiery
dragons policy' "washed its hands totally of the mugs"
and harmony was resumed again. I mean with the
English Shakesburt Company at my side I can make a
church choir hum with pride. Did I not obtain footage of
crowds cheerin' the Pope in '83 for background noise in
the ESC's upper crusty *Coriolanus* by Shakesburt?
That's Splott poise and punctilio all over, can't beat it.
Never mind if "the bilingual bleatin's of solar powered
bins" kept half the population awake, we never lost our
equilibrium. Then dammo again, just when refinement
was gettin' the upper hand, immoral bacteria flopped
out, yes, in Swansea town again. This was The Demon
Drink Deluge mixed with the university's Plague of
Plagiarism.

**Charm is uphill work sometimes, but in Swansea,
it's like labourin' in Siberian quarries.**

See, Swansea's nite spots rocketted to numbers
beyond computation "due to the excessive willingness
of magistrates to grant licenses." Jockstrap urged 'no sot
areas' 'cos of the continuin' 25,000 drunks disgorged on
Saturday nights. But in the middle of his dry crusade,

Swansea's most futuristic Club, *Sloanes,* got voted 'Disco of the Year', UK wide, what shame. "A feather in the hat of brewer-run premises" they said, but I think not. Where's the true allure there I ask you, the charm, the calm of perfect harmony? Hah, don't come near me Mr Sloane!

*Head of Meic the Mighty with white Washer*

Then it was the Swans tum to be copycat. In the university philosophy department it was. Here students was admitted "without references or interview." Nor intelligence by the sound of it. And after three years of swannin' (guess the origin of that lazy little word!) they got degrees for "not handin' in essays" and, if they did, "the dissertations was 43% copied direct from text books in a patchwork of styles with 100 spelling and grammatical errors". And, if worse even, "the marks was bumped up to pass" and these very dodgy lads was MA'd on the spot when they'd really failed outright overnight. But I was invited in again, like here tonight, to speak with breedin' and enlightenment in their Senate House on the over-generous pedagogues of Socrates and Wittgenstein. "Just a by-product of over-hasty preparation," I chided the turncoat lecturers good naturedly, "your accusations are a soupcon off in this day of Yuppee affability". I pointed out, rather handsomely I thought, that "they were responsible for denigration of colleagues, breaches of confidence and disruption of college life." But the donkeys brayed on and the whole silliness now resides with the Department of Trade and Fisheries where it belongs, it pongs enough. Did he acquit himself with honour? I hear you ask. Well, ratherish must be my modest answer, for you see before you a well-hung chappie unspoiled by vanity or lechery. Yes.

Those disturbed lecturers, see, corrupted by the facts had broached the real but unsung national anthem of Wales called "Please Don't Make a Wave." Our doubtin' Thomases, understand, are graduates of Discretion and never learn one bloody lesson!

Then Dame Queezy Aimless, England's firstclass third-rater - a novelist some argue – foolishly insisted that the Welsh Education Committe "fixed results." What lingo there? Nothing dainty about "fixed" is there? What about' grace' or 'favour' or 'simple humanity', bloody Aimless? Then he accused Wales's N.O.D. (NumberOneDeadman) Dylan Thomas of bein' "a pernicious carpetpisser." Not a cordial comment I thought, the yellow sod. I mean how could he say that

243

when a statue of Captain Cat, the most lovable character in the world, had just been unveiled on Abernathy Quay? This on a Marina where "stony stories' trails lead (well-mannered) tourists to all the carved figures of the town, the wall texts, steel and metal features, architectural glass and the 120 ft by 40 ft non-chemical mural image of Dylan himself," while artist D. Weaver done "handmade busts of Dylan" and framed "quality poems" by him for the personable guests in the Dylan Tea Rooms. Put that up your pipe, Dame Aimless, you never wrote one line of poetry in your bluddy life! Moreover the Dylan Thomas Theatre made Dylan Thomas even more internationally famouser with a play called *Dylan Thomas,* which was then exported to Hong Cong by the Merlyn Theatre Company and tickets was raffled for a crate of Dylan Thomas Champagne. Why not? Life is a bundle of sticky things and is brightened by a sense of fun.

**What about table manners, you ask? Well, just this - no elbows, see, I'm warnin' you - all joints on table will be carved!**

Feminine ladies got the hots for immortality too. Kate Dunne done the First Voice in *Under MilkPudding* in radiant girl tones and Jess Wilson, one of the "put out poetesses," done a dernier cri film, *Portrait of the Artist as an Older Woman.*

**Yes, salute the risin' graces of Splott But, yes, sweety charmers out there tonight, remember what ladies do at leisure time. Upholstery is timeless.**

**Grass too remains paramount in the countryside as you picnic, and flower arranging is never to be sneezed at, especially if those gay gypsophila and pittosporom blooms are fixed up just a bit, well, Marie Antoinettish! Just thought I'd mention it!**

Then dammo again, Dame Queezy's bitty novel *The Old Devils* turned up in Tobyobe's Mold Theatre disguised as a play' cos it had lots of Welsh pricks in. Tobyobe swore he "was impressed by the humanity of it all," a play wherein "men carouse at the Bible and Black, women sip Soave at ten. This on an open space, almost an abbatoir:" The characters comported like "Greek Godesses and the Furies, and they actually destroyed Alan Weaver." Cwmdonkin Drive? More like Cwmbonkin' Drive to me, and what's new about that? And who's this "Alan Weaver'.' anyway? Serve him right! Tobyobe's final message to the world was, "within this pain, this turmoil and stirring of guts, there is a sense of re-birth." That is Splotspoke at its best! Tobyobe learned his creed from us: 'if it is incomprehensible use it, but use it beautifully - like a creep!'

Two tiny notes of maladroitness crept in but they was soon swept under the carpet. Mrs Harris who had donated *Scenes of Pembrokeshire* found them on the floor of the Dylan Thomas Museum "in bits, with sinister liquid poured on." Listen Mrs Harris, talk of the floral decorations, ask the Curator gently, "Do you bike?" But do not mention "sinister liquids" s. v. p. it only upsets the gels. But the most indelicate cut of all was an ill-bred bounder of a tramp who tried to sell phials of 'Dylan sweat' in Swansea's Salubrious Passage but try as he might, he was soon railroaded out of town. Jockstrap & Ilk Inc. soon saw to that. And you know, lovely one and all here, try as I might too, after all this time on my mind I cannot sweeten that tramp's lyin' little cup. Then, all is forgiven Swans! They done a blissful thing: declared themselves Wales' Most Premiere City of Culture and promulgated a special Bull, *Percent for All,* a bloomin' appeal to developers "to think pretty" and to theatre companies to launch a "mouth-waterin' menu of avantgardism" to counter them soiled dunes and damaged goods academe. They smells more fragranter already, right?! The response was instant. The Hampsters played in Cwmtwrch at Taffy's Trash Venue, and featured the electrifying Snail's Pace Slim. *Elena and Robert* was done prompt by Gundi Ellert, translated by Tinch Minter, performed by the Wilde Players. With another 80 turns all round town, with some rejected mind to avoid last year's "irritatin' clashes of similar events" especially at the same venues. So with the thoroughbred Swans at the very apex of their good groomin', their beau gestes pumpin' hands like mad, healthy civic spirit suddenly went down the w.c. again, dammo! The Swans irritatin' 25,000 urine-bohemians rolled in with their *Beer Festival* at the Dame Patti Pavilion, what a come down again! And where - to put it without du1cetry - "mind-bendin' brews was dispensed". Like diabolic Moulden's *Black Adder* Ale, for example, *Son-of-a-Bitch* Bitter (from Penarth's Bull Mastiff Brewery), while famous heinous Crown Buckley's Beers offered a steamin' brew called most blasphemiously *The Reverend L. James Original* Ale. Felinfoel and Brain's best threw in its *Double Dragon*

Tipple and sent those wicked 25,000 rabble reelin' home to their sties.

O Dewi 'Sodom' Davies, 0 Minister 'Lulu' Rearden, 0 Councillor 'Jockstrap' Lewis, sometimes I am forced to confess that Swansea needs your prayers more than my ample charms.

Then Cardiff done not her best. Opened a new play she did, with a tin opener, thus launching Wales' new ear-drum bustin' *Theatre of Screech*. It started up innocent like enough with them Polish Group Avakum who at first cheered us up with "fundamentalist orgies and pagan mass suicides by candlelight" and actors "gnashin' their teeth, foamin at the mouth, hangin' from poles, exposin' the old titties," (What's new under the globe I ask?) "rockin' cribs, and finally gettin' stuck in huge loaves of bread." Not all bad then, but Cardiff's Lords of Misrule stuck in their dishevelled oar and the usually impeccable Brif Cof went into "an orgy of corrugated iron, dustbin lids, buckets, shopping trollies, while actors in mini-leotards sprayed audiences with H20." One reviewer roared inaudibly when a trolley smashed into his knee-cap and reflected, "I knew then it was time to leave" and limped over to Cardiff's New Theatre, 'the closest thing to heaven in Wales,' where he was last seen revellin' in traditional values and moral re-armament in the presence of a well-spoken Enid Bagnold play. He later wrote of Shakesburt's *Measure for Measure:* "Tho' the language was archaic, it was at least ethical," testament to his miraculous powers of recovery.

Let me disclose to you now, without ado, this gamey scriber was straight out of Splot, my Splot Academy, home of undisguised gallantry and elegance!

Yes, dammo this pestilence of Screech spread to Cardiff's *Winterval III* with its "clatter of rollerskaters, stilt walkers" and, thank God for some relief, winsome girl actresses "performin' in rubber rings." But then Splot's etiquette went out of the window and the cast went haywire with it, boundin' on stage "with jittery footwork" and comportin "like a rugby team on corrugated sheets with lethal jagged edges" while the Ronnie Barkertype scenes displayed lack of soul and vocal rhythm. Finally "bongo drums drowned out the finest text in the English Language." Yes, ye moist Academes of Wales, that was Shakesburt's *Romeo and Juliet* for you! Exorcise it please, Dewi 'Sodom' Davies with bell, book and hatchet! Fun-lovin' Director Mike.James afterwards hinted, "I didn't want to cloud the play. I wanted the music of the words." WelL my Mikey, you won't find it if your actors screech like owls on top of other owls. Ten to twenty in Splott's elocution cells for you, Mikey!

Then the Directors, notably Augusto Boal and Eugenio Barba, at the Performing Arts Centre in Cardiff, realized that the *Theatre of Screech* was due mainly to profoundly empty Directors themselves, 75 per cent of whom Mr Gulbenkian had discovered in his exaggerated report had never been directly trained in any branch of theatre at all. To obviate this obvious long-standin' gangrene, Perrormmg Arts started up the most subtle directors' course in history, takin' in "bi-annual modules... restructerization guinea-pig models... interactive scenographers... performance fragments."

*Anattomia del Attore* with Zygmunt Moliti, Ludwig Flaszen *Giving Voice* on confrontationalist shamanism, Martini Buzacott in *Age of Terror* revealin' that love of theatre betrays a fundamental failing in man. All meaningless junk but luscious for multi-lingual subsidy. Bravo, directors of Wales, corrugated sheet-flatteners all! But all was not foetid! Judith Fitzalan Alan urged OJ} her *Seaman's Return* with the Bay's All Star Welsh Sikh Tigers. Dance Alive done their noble fable *Pockets Knotted* with "dancers in crinolines like pomanders of popcorn" all moving "to a Scarlatti sonata, gracefully or vulture like, with well-toned limbs." Tone on, 0 Dance Alive! ye learned your body vibes from Splot! No more noisome was Denise Deegan's play *No Birds Sing* which had Welsh only spoken after an ice-cap melted - God knows what they spoke before - and Frank Vickery done thrillin' work with *All' s F air* where star Sophie's gravy-browned legs wowed 'em. The Prince of Wales re-opened as a glitzy disco and all hopes for a Welsh national theatre there went up in a puff of bingo! In the north in Tobyobe's pit in Denbigh, Adzido's Pan Africans "revealed the vastness of the Dark Continent as never before." The natives of Ffestiniog responded likewise and them Zulu warriors quailed in terror! Then the most engagin' New Word Dance Company done *The Bundle Boogie Woogies* and *The Dinosaur's Knee.* OK, but this comeback of family values was a bit marred by Hi Jinx puttin' on "the most depressin' play in the world," *Paradise Drive,* which was "absolute hell." But

249

Tobyobe made us all gurgle again with his *Heads Turn as the Hunt Goes By* with "famous figures like Sir Walter Raleigh and the teenage spy Chris Marlowe stabbed in the eye at twenty nine." "This ambitious world," chanted Tobyobe, "turned out its finest." Aye.

Then under the influence of Splot's instant spiritual *Godspray,* Margam Park's stupendous one hundredth and seventieth Passion Play, with over 180 teetotal actors, all there was in Wales, was squashed on. Local goverment officer Peter Davies "was nervous but honoured" tv be Jesus hisself and was soon adept, in Splott' s best equine tuition, at mountin' the Lords donkey called Bandit and then bein' strapped to a ten-foot cross like a real actor. "Natural darkness coincided with the crucifixion" which continued until June the 24th. Spectators from Canada was even gapin' there.

Then something hellish happened which brushed aside all thespian endeavour, curbed both climax and anti-climax, and halted Keltic Kultur in its trax. A total and utter stalwart of Welsh Poesy went and quit hisself with immediate effect. This was Splott's Number One and Only WACO Alumnus, the man who got the most golden opinions of hisself in the world, a legend in his own toilet, that fine Terminator of Welsh Literature, Meic 'Golden Boy' Stephens. Oh God! Out he went, and this in spite of "strict codes and procedures" (you can have a copy) which were completely ethical, open and correct and never inquorate. "Rubbish!" as Cross Word Man, Tom 'Rubbish' Owen, master supremo of WACO, glitteringly hissed. "Why," continued he, "Wales supports experimental theatre more than anywhere in Britain!" So poop on ye blatherin' Saxon thespians outside of Offa's Dyke, now ye know. Knightly 'Rubbish' Owen has spoke!

Yes, the birds in the trees outside WACO's Tour Ivoire HQ ceased their sweet jargoning and statues of crocodiles on the Green wept real tears! "Why, 0 why?" the universe moaned, "why didour Golden Boy, havin' voted himself into his job for life, then went and voted himself out for life?" Why did he so disdain still more sweet junketings to Minsk and frog Quebec, why did he repulse so many pension benefits, tasty perks of paper clip and yards of broadband, endless editorial tips and trips, author's laundry lists (for a mere song) and those beery central heatin' seminars up the Rhine? All went and for what? The company of the dubious sparrows in his garden? Oh God, at last we must all ask, was this the action of a PRA T?

I must confess that, with all my old chummy chum chums and old boy nets about me, no one in Wales knows the why or the wherefore of this abrupt rotten-abcess self-extraction which left Golden Boy toothless to the gales of life. No supergrass or jailbird songster knew "nuthin' guvnor" neither. No smelly Gas Board mogul, University Press Repectable, Reverend or Lecturer, Welsh Office Righteous Titan or even one BBC TV Prolix Head, ever gossiped about it or had the faintest inklin' why the Golden Boy had got hisself by the scruff of his own neck and chucked hisself out of the top drawer, pissin' on delectable power with oaths and glares of contempt at the world. But ·lovesome Meic, after all still our main Companion by, with and from Welsh Literature ($1,195 per copy) did modestly quip upon his playful, slitherin' exit, "I have had along and successful career with WACO. *Poetry Wales* is the most prestigious periodical in Britain and was founded by me. After poet Harri Webb had helped me with it, he found his voice. We laugh a lot. 0 yes, I have projects." Ha, hal A most valium valedictory, Golden Boy, but watch out for the 13th disciple, Bill 'Yaweh' Anderton, Chief Manchester's Greatest Constable. Yes, God chooses his own victims just like you chose yours, Boy, but first God makes them mad.

But WACO's Cross Word Man Tom 'Rubbish' Owen and top kick Matty 'Three Thousand Acres' Pritchardo riposted on cue with the usual drivels and smokescreens, exclaimin' that WACO's grant had gone up from 8.95 million dollops to 9.9 million dollops and in a tellin' aside, slick red herrin' there, Matty hoyo, praised the imperishable Moving Bein' and all Welsh Theatre Companies for goin' allover the known world and for havin' "a strong future and international venues" and reminded the whole of mankind that "Wales had come from the bottom to the phenomenal" which had "dispelled myths by and large and the drawbacks of business markets." Tom 'Rubbish' and 'Three Thousand Acres' concluded with knowledge aforethought, "private investment is the key to auditorium."

**But still we demand, "Why oh why, hast thou forsaken us, 0 Golden Boy? Why this so unnecessary self-deprivation? We cannot even defecate without thoughts of thee!"**

But WACO finally put its foot down with a firm hand and ended all speculation with, "A Company must first set out its stall for core funds, for the danger is there may be a van Gogh out there." WACO's financial

Master Malign chimed in, "We are very pleased, no further erosion." And the Institute of Welsh Affairs backed this sodden officialese with more cotton wool, "new centres, arts festivals, chamber orchestras, choral skills and 75,000 pound go-aheads" all there for the graspin'. But Tom 'Rubbish' asserted back that "the uplift" was "too poor to bridge the gap" in spite of "the rollin' programme" for all in all "just a little push would be catastrophic" and "sourness still stared them in the face." With a phenomenal staff of over 65, however, the National Audit Off ice did mention a bit about a helluva lots of surplus bods swannin' about WACO and did remark on WACO's odd sense of efficiency. But no one from WACO was available for comment, especially our Golden Boy, by now outside shiverin' in the cold from grossly reduced importance and wonderfully diminished dollops. Tom 'Rubbish' finally shrugged off all suspicion of anything to do with skull duggery anywhere on planet earth, and kinda grinned with almost Splottlike insouciance, "I wouldn't be able to sleep if! hadn't done the Times crossword."

But this talk of grand cash meant tite sphincter time for Tobyobe who desired "urgent action to stave off short-fall over-spendin' s" mainly due to *The Revenger's Tragedy* whjch lost vast audiences due to the inexplicit rape scenes. Same embarrassment at the Torch Theatre Milford, too, whose "vivid presence" and "enormous panache" could not conceal an overpowerin' deficit.

Come to Splott, ye halt, ye lame, bring me your huddled sheets, bring all you got, we'll show you how to charm milk out of a churn! We'll show WACO together just why they can't "pull the plug at peak periods on this focal point of cultural activities." I tell you, lovelies, didn't Splott fix Movin' Bein's 200,000 dollops for convertin' turn-of-the-century Saint Stephen's into a centre of "counter culture avant gardism"! This we did and so sophisticated like it was fackin' smashin', and Movin' Bein' was celebrated from smoky Essen to the sun-drenched, luxurious sierras of Nebraska. True.

Then divine Movin' Bein', only too conscious of the recedin' role of hollow directors, on our basic advice, transformed its mainly body-writhing' shows to "highly politicised text-based vehicles" (plays?) "in the fallow year." Very civil of them I thought because I agree "the value of images has been undermined by marketin' people who use the whole history of art to sell things." So Movin' Bein' went and proved it with their ten thousand-year-old *Mabinogion* and *The Continental Coffee House Show.* Listen now, since we're up to our debts in Europe, a bit of a tip for you, gratis. Note the French. When in Rome…


**Look, now, see when you're all alone at home at dinner, always fold the napkin when you're finished, but in a foreign hotel abroad, always crumple it up and toss it aside like a soiled glove. Like that! Try it, there in the front row. Yes, that's it. There's lovely!**

254

*Welsh Arts Council Spokesperson issues a statement*

Listen now, with, such upright propriety on the rise, things always go better and they did with O'Neil at the Sherman' cos Neil' d wrote 'Cardiff' in the title of his play *Bound East for Cardiff.* And following WACO's lead in global poise, Theatre Taliesin done *Routes and Leaves* "to resist the McDonaldisation of the world." Then some other very feminine enchantresses done *Under the Skin* "to resist monoculture." Meantime the Sherman's New Hit Leader, Phil Clark, Welsh, transformed the theatre "from imminent death" and done a hard-hittin' poem *V* on English class values, then forged ahead with the play - sod the film! - "the searingly courageous" *My Beautiful Laundrette* to cross the class barrier too with a social mix. Then Dannie *Abse'sAsh on a Young Man's Sleeve* was tapped into the ashtray of the stage' cos it was a novel much more famouser than all of Dannie's plays, however fine, which went undone of course. This fresh approach guaranteed a 200,000 dollop foyer conversion, and why not? You scratch my foyer, I'll scratch... Geddit? Yes, chuckle along with me! Richard Gough next got tough with his Theatre of Non Literature. His Practical Company done *The Burnin' o/the Dancers* and threw in *Symposia on Theatre Anthropology* (watch those apes, Dickie, boyo!) pressed on with *Nature and Ideologies* - snappy title there - all done right in front of "renowned guests" so they could "spark each other off." Old Roger the Dodger 'Jargoneer' Tomlinson at once offered to do a most winnin' 274,173 dollop "Report on the 15 to 25 age group." AfterwhichCeri 'Gift-of-Tongues' Sherlock, "who knows Welsh, Russian, Greek, Hebrew, Italian and German by heart and does not suffer fools gladly", girded up his auxiliaries and decamped for London with his Multi-Gerund Company. After this, plays and players spilled out of every crook and nanny. Tobyobe dumped in with Festival III, *The Birth of Merlin* or *The Chi/de who Knew his Father,* played by appealin' Roy

Huddas Merlin who "cracked pre-Arthurian jokes To pre-Arthurian people" while near him fascinatin' Anna Karen done *J oan-Go-To-It* with total romp-con-peachy brio straight out of Splot. Then not so Silly Billy Gilly Adams grasped the mythic *Branwen* "by the scruff of the neck too, shook it free of much of its magic and mystery and transformed it into Third World Dictatorships and the contemporary Irish Problem." The set was two pylons representin' opposite Kingdoms, 'cept the King of Ireland "looked like a mediaeval wrestler" but the girl harlequin done the humour nice. Then even more radiant girl sisters done *The Women of 13 Shirts,* each shirt posted in, see, "generated songs, poems and dances." But the venimous reviewer sent the whole lot to the laundry: "a mish-mash of cacophonous warblings, told in outer Mongolian." Most of the audience was asleep "when one girl gave birth to a hot water bottle while another washed a Mexican chemise". These enticin' oops girls ended with "headless dancin' to the tune of *Fallin' in Love with Love".*

The Sherman's next *Celebration* was not neither, whatever they say. Then more dolly-bird darlin' s come back with the XPG Company and done *The Adult Dead Child* and *It's a Girl* with "five pregnant ladies chainin' themselves to a nuclear waste disposal undertakin' against hypocrisy and big business." Then trim Anna Readman's *Hard Core,* a Polish solidarity play set in ancient Rome in a simulated sex brothel, hit hard.

But to retum to *Celebrations.* About a weddin' or a funeral it was, but "the cast had conversations among themselves due to more bein' on stage than in the audience and the reviewer called time at last when a drinkin' chum of Arthur excused the Captain for not going to the funeral because he had collapsed into a bowl of disinfectant in the pub lavatory."

But, listen, with just one minute of our Xmas Shakesburt Hypnosis Tutorial *Grab Success by the Neck and Never Let itGo, Celebrations* would have mesmerized a bucket of delirious eels! Likewise G.B. Shaw's *The Widower's House* at The Torch which "dropped with a dull and awkward thud" accordin' to one local auctioneer "because few people enjoy bein' lectured at with antique sermons on Victorian property developers." Listen, with us on the job, Mr Auctioneer, them droopy longeurs of Shaw and Sophockles got no hope. So send in for details, don't put off suspense no longer. Listen now to a bit of inside dope. It will take you straight to the Lord Mayor's banuqet table. When invited to dine, do not scrape every scrap of your avocado out. Always leave a bit of a morceau inside - for Mr Manners, right? Yes, such salad touches always helps in the gut-retchin' scramble to the top soiree. But pity the Standard Telephone Companydone a *Kismet* "that begged to be pruned," and Eugenio Barba who done Danish Odin Teatret's *Seminal Groups* "in lab-like Groteski conditions." Judith went on "to behead a cruel Assyrian general" and *The Origin of Table Manners* proved once and for all, that "there is only a thin veneer of civilization." *Amadeus* in Aber proved he was "no burping buffoon" and the Torch come on with *Cluendo* "with six surprise endin's". Tobyobe introduced *An Enemy of the People* from Norway 'cos there's no problems in Wales like cottage burnin' which no Welsh playwright in his tiny mind could write up anyway. In

Glasgow's Tramway, a Welsh jugular version of *J ekyll and Hyde* went on, with Pakistani actors. The Earth Fall Dancers dropped in with *The Secret Soul of Things,* swirlin' with martial arts and Bulgarian bagpipes. Brif Cof topped it all with *Pax,* "an ecological flyin' circus in a simulated Gothic Cathedral of 40ft scaffoldin." Five naked dancers done "aerial ballet," then come back "as angels creepin' through holes in the ozone layer crawlin' wordlessly over the audience to warrn all persons about it, then was winched back up to Paradise" and flew off to be unforgettable again in Essen, Barcelona and the New World. To help out, Theatre Taliesin sailed back with the discovery of the USA before the Vikings, with Prince Madoc surrounded by Indo Jazz Fusions, the Sioux nation, Keltic Reels and Punjabi Bhangra. The poem *Gododdin* was done "scenographic ally" among "specially designed sand, trees and wrecked cars in a large circle gradually flooded with continuous tapes from the Car Test Dept." Yes, all these - and more - we made them into Young Peoples Projects Everyone Could Understand and Love.

**And don't ever forget, it's only Splott can teach you how to comport proper when you offers an unknown lady an umbrella – even when it's not rainin'.**

So now you know again, last of the Eighties and first of the Nineties had little to do as usual with a native Welsh theatre. Wise beyond his columns, journalist David Fanning astutely noted, "Playwriting and theatre have well rooted traditions in Wales, witness the countless actors, directors and writers who have contributed so much to British and world theatre." But top politico Dr Kim Howells MP wailed that "Wales has no theatrical tradition at all. Theatre is a poor relation." Dramatist Elaine Morgan put him wrong, "There *are* good dramatists!" Then put him right again: "Wales has no theatrical tradition." Not so Silly Billy Gilly Adams this time squeaked, "Welsh theatre fails by committee," then rallied, "new plays are more exciting for people than people realize." And she should know for this lady Dame Aimless has written not a single one in her interminable one thousand year theatrical· career, Between poems 'of astonishing beauty, top poetico Bob Minhinnick ventured, "Wales, in terms of drama is... er... a bit of awasteland." Other arts boss functionaries prayed that the Made in Wales Theatre Company "would never be influenced by small town attitudes." But how can this be when their minds are meaner than the smallest village in the land? And how can the dramatists claim to be more than offensive foulmouthed provincial garbage dispensers when they are treated so shabbily by those very agencies which are meant to improve their lot - the preenin' academics and their dead literature departments, the W ACOs in their florid and undrained Museum swamp; the local worthies grovellin' to alien genius toads, the spendthrift directors? These sordid, cross-eyed wonders never cease. But listen now, Attar of Roses is still here. You can easy ignore the piddlin' gripes of unadulterated playwrights like Frank Vickery who nagged away that even when his play was extended by public demand he only got "85 pathetic dollops and not a cent of the normal seven and a half per cent of box." On he drivelled, "under these circumstances I don't think I'm going back to the Sherman." Sullen brute! Don't he know in our book self-denial is its own reward, not his. Vickery should be so lucky. If he was under former director 'Ostrich Egg' Axleworthy, he wouldn't have got a stale pork pie! Then more uncouth, uppity, ungrateful playwrights whinged on.

After WACO urged the publication of playscripts and Hallmark Books done plays by Mark Jenkins and Tim Green, they most offensively demanded, "Why should book publishers receive up to 50% of our box office receipts?" Hallmark admitted "this was a problem," and are still ponderin', sly boots, "how playwrights might obtain a proper share." So, too, TVs *Art and Soul* mentioned in passin' "there was over 201 playwrights in Wales and only 1.01 in performance." But bluddy well so what? Sounds about right to me. Take no notice

Then David Fannin' went all meek like, just right again: "There are no bardic chairs for dramatists." So *sotto voce* no one gave a second solitary fart. But I mean, to be straight, what's the point if Fannin' urges a long term strategy for drama if Vickery or Green or Dee Jones got egg stains on their ties and reeks like billy goats? Those suited person silhouettes of City Hall and Varsity recoils natural-like anyroad when them biro lumpens looms on the horizon. Them dire twerps should learn to keep their opinions like their egg stains to their crumblin' selves. But Fannin' with his new nice line in mildness fluttered on, "Why is WACO a law unto itself and answerable to no one?" Wonder fine, boyo, if you toe the line! Why don't those pliable scribes. Taffy manipulatables after all, just realize, like grown ups, that Greed always rides roughshod and rises over Everyman unstoppable as a slag heap slidin' on a cemetery. Next that actual English ninny-iconclast John Pick was totally futile in his book of tantrums *Vile Jelly* - the jelly bein' the Arts Council of GB no less. Poke it out with a dry stick he wants, like the eye in Shakesburts *Leer,* and watch that squishy orb carried out on tides of sewage - ugh! —subsidies that WACO dumped deliberate out there! - sick Pick says! Huh! I mean if you chucked them rosy WACOs out, they'd be muggin' you an' me personal on the streets. No, let 'em stay and rob the tax payer in secret in their marble halls. Far safer that way for all humanity I say.

But a word to the worst now. Hark you old dramatists, your onlyhope in plays to come is our Charm Seminary in Splot, don't you see? I promise you we can teach you how to bend the knee and bare the gums with panachee in the most appealin' lap-dog manner. Look what we done with Cardiff's New Theatre herself. They got diplomats as doormats there now and they don't come cheap. Yes, we even learned a theatre how to smile! Little flea-bite bods like you is sprats to us. Come to our portals, mortals, and be big!

**Another social debacle is them scribes has never been learned which way to tip the old soup plate or to hang the toilet paper, proper see. Always with the free sheet danglin' facin' outwards towards the eager hand, like that, see. And the soup plate always tipped away, see. Yes, that's how you handles the old soul of boop, gents.**

Once youn done that like you an' me, you all could be invited to the most fsmousest and most fashionablest hostesses in Upper Lands, Swansea, and make the most precious small talk about it, like all our graduates of parlez vous! No more tradesman's entrance if you bends an ear. Enroll now, boyos, and banish forever, mind as well as body odours. You can be as ingratiatin' as a WACOman on the double-take!

But surprisin' like, London's not in WACOs gift and there in the Great Wen, the morbid bacilluses of Gwalia rose to the surface like turds that won't flush away. Take this *SPUD* excrescence:

*Society for the Prevention of Unnecessary Directors.* How silly! For failures envious of the gravy train. I mean without all our directors all the Arts Councils of the land could not exist. Directors are Wales's yes-men of the ages and their brown-nose epics fill Reading Rooms of pages. Why don't these threadbare pen-pushers drop jealousy of us, once and for all? I beg them all, still good humouredly too, apply now. Get out of overdraft into overdrive with the charm of old world Splott. Don't wait, don't hesitate, talent's too late if you can't flog it, mate. But all this fair play from US mattered not one jot 'cos disgruntled, displaced playwrights like Tim Green and Ed Thomas still fled to London with their Gradual Decline Company - what a name, what an admission of defeat! And another Company called The Company. How borin', where's the genius in that? Oops, pardon. See what I mean by effluvia bein' wind-borne!

There was more stuff. The Plays from Wales Company was in the Strand with *Black Book on the*

*Welsh Theatre Four* wrote by that dullard- braggart Dedwydd Jones, hysterical dolt out of Dyfed. And that Young Turk Kenneth Griffith - like to take the mick out of him, come on Special Branch! - acted it out, a la bravura it was said. But that cannot be, the material of *Black Book IV* is scrappy crappy coffee table fare. Taffo Keith Baxter (Joan Collins's leadin' man) and his play *Barnaby and the Old Boys* was done at the Vaudeville, again for some sinister reason inthe Taff-Bog of The Strand. That lyin' journal *The, Stage* said it was a treat. Misguided twats, ring Splot next time,- well put you mighty righty! After all when *Barnaby* went on in Mold, north Wales, the locals spotted it at once. "Blasphemious!" they cried. They got its putrid measure fine, God bless em! But baffled Baxter said this was "the only time he had been invited back to Wales and that come from an Englishman." As if that was any excuse. Bluddy racist. Some of my best friends here are white settlers from Surrey.

Then off the arch heresiarch Baxter swaggered, invited by New York to unveil a plaque in the White Horse tavern to our N.O.D, Dylan Thomas. Actor Windsor Davies, also on The Strand (got to be the centre of that Taff conspiracy), said a Welsh National Theatre "could only find a home on the streets of London." Another blasphemer of what is finest, dang him!

See, its Splott's philosophers give Wales's crach (scab or establishment) three witchin' words to put down all writer-gripers. These three go: "You left Wales!" Repeat after me, "You left Wales! So piss off!" Say it again! Music to their tears! "Piss off!" The sweet wisdom behind this bein' if you live one inch over the border, you're a turncoat and out of order! Covers a multitude of rejections, especially if there's only work over the border. Oh high irony! Chuckle along with me! But listen, sadly other malefic cultures floated on the surface of Mid Glam with its oil patch, Cardiff town. Tim Green's *Peerless Jim Driscoll,* Mark Jenkin's *Birthmarks and Burton* (Burton bein' Wales's N.T.D. - Number Two Great Deadman) Peter Lloyd's *Scam,* Lawrence Allan's *A Blow to Bute Street,* Tony Conran's *Branwen,* *CharlesWay's!nBleakMidwinter,* Sean Mathias's *Prayer for Wings,* among other repellant trailin' weeds of plays. But relief to report, these pieces are now' mostly rottin' away in bags of London mail. Curse their steamin' compost, don't they realize there's more to Welsh creativity than the futile fleshpots of popular London success? I tell you - ssh! - what we really aim at is to make them all yell out with chagrin in their eyes, "For God's sake, get me out of Wales!" Look homeward angels now, the most heroic note of all. You must all go and gaze with fixed eye and slack jaw at our new central hall with its recently unveiled lists of alumni and their most famed accomplishments. You will learn with awe just who Splott and its Socrateses have encouraged to bugger off out of Wales throughout the ages, from N.O.D. Dylan Thomas (we helped him out of life as well) to Richard Burton, N.T.D., to liverish Dedwydd Jones, even worse, he lives still. The shitwit! The twatnut!

But nine-hundred per cent by God will continue to be escorted to the Bristol Suspension Bridge.

Look at our age-old success rate: the first Tudor, Henry VII, to Lloyd George. Why, now you know! It was old Splotty who screwed them so they turned their back on Wales forever and could be blamed for it in perpetuity! "You left Wales!" Piss off! Try that! See how they run! Easy as pluckin' a fuckin' daffodil, right? But apart from these prime Ejectors and Ejectments, we could not have been so victorious without our HQ Pink Gin Brigadiers on the homeless front. At the goin' down of the sun read just a few of our honour lists of Heroes of Expulsion: Councillor 'Jockstrap' Lewis, Clive 'Whirling Dervish' Barnes, Cross Word Man, Tom 'Rubbish' Owen, Grant' Indignation' Williams, Jimmy 'Green Tree' Evans, (distinguished genius there), Alan 'The Colossus-of-the-Short-Stemmed-Pipe' Williams, Mayor 'We-Want-To:-Be-Famous' Lloyd, 'Three Thousand Acres' Prichardo, 'Ostrich Egg' Axleworthy, Shakesburt 'Prince of Egg' and many others too worthy to mention!

I'd also like to announce now that we are in trainin' for the next election and I tell you this - we'reaimin' for the very summit once again and again this time. Next year on this platform you will see PM Neil Kinnock if necessary, and failin' him, PM Major John Somebody, and failin' him, the Swans' own 'Tarzan' PM Heseltine and failin' him, a jar of vaseline. But whoever it may be I can promise thee, ye will find behind them all, your Chief Charmer here, unholy ME! And behind me the whole suave storm troopers of Splott who can sweeten any bad report in the land and knock spots off any truth in hand. Let no one here grow bigger than his jackboots for he'll have to deal with a me robbed of all geniality. Be leery, deary, is the order of the day! And behind all these Hypnotic Leaders, hidden in highly sensitive arsenals, we have huge reserves of the most precious bull and bullion Wales has to offer to the world - magazines of sweatin' servility, cannons of explosive hypocrisy and gigantic powder barrels of mediocrity. All waitin' to extinguish any spark of genius or originality forever and a day. Again and again and again - hooray!

Yes we are the past, present and future masters of all right-thinkin' principalities and powers - ours. That's why this lavender and roses can of worms in my hand is mere baggy tell. Smell it now, go on! See! Perfume to my ears. The report gleams pure as leprosy tho' it pongs of roses all the way.

To conclude on this enchanted evenin', always repeat every day our Academy's Prize Commandment: "Never ask questions to which there could be embarrassin' answers." Once you never ask that, you'll never ask any thin'. You'll be on your way and all will be well with your flannelette Wales.

**One last itty bitty word of advice to the cuddly girl debbies here. Now see how I just dropped my hanky? Well, imagine, there you are in a classic mini at the old Ambassador's Royal Reception, surrounded by stars of screen and stage. How to pick up that inadvertent snot-rag on the deck is the breathless question. How? Well, with the delectable comporteement of Splott, of course. I'll demonstrate. Like this, with knees together, and parallel to all those fab guesties. See, point is not with gapin' thighs splayed open, like that, so all can see your undoubted super undergrowth. I mean no flashin' the old mons veneris of man's desirin', right? So girlies, try that when you gets home tonight, you luscious debbie**

webbies. Knees together, however randy wandy you feels. So at any time at your next Reception, at, say, the Palace of Versails, you'll never have a single moment of hanky spanky embarrassment in your life. Knees bend, knees bend, ha, ha, ha! All aboard the gravy train of Splott, chuff, chuff, hoot, hoot, see you next weekend at The Fisherman's Friend in the romantic duomos of the gay Seychelles.

*(Disruption at back of auditorium)*

What's that... ? What... ? Who... ? Those yobboes back there? Put down those ach y fi pens, is it?

Obscene ink now is it? You dare! The drips, ach, stop! Who let em in? Help! Stormy Troopers storm in! Charm School Suffocators, press on! WACOmen remove their subsidies! Excellent, no bruises, but what a load of balls! Do your dirtiest, don't worry, our Lord Chief Injustices are at hand! Worthymen heroes of Splott. Golden Boy Terminators of class of twenty-two, Meic, arrive! Get those soddin' fuckers outta in here before they start writin' all over the place and underminin' an otherwise perfectly respectable session of us. Ge 'em out! I wanna see multiple ejections! "Ejections" I said. Bums! Do it! Dammo, dare you raise your pens at me! Police coppers on you then! Call in the Scotland Yard Corruption squad right now! Hold back, you paper scribblin' louts! Now folks, I may be rushin' off on my hands and knees, but note that famous crooked smile of Splott's still in its rightful place! Even in extreemis like this, I avoid the wooden stare of unsociability. My snow-drop report still smells as sweet as any navel. No fluff about it! Mission bluddy well done. Brilliant, top boyo of Splott! Don't weep all, I'll be back, often as hell! There's a whole new generation of sleepers in the audience, heartfelt allies all the way, numb bum zombies of Wales. Whee, wheee, whee, there's pee for thee! Now piss off out of my charming life!

*(Exit the CHARMER sniffing the report, swooning with delight)*

---

**Breaking News** – read all about it!:

The Taffo-Contagion 'theatre bureaucracy' has spread across Offa's Dyke into Albion itself, without benefit of quarantine, especially in built up areas. The single full-length play for main stages is on the brink of extinction! With no more directors who favour the old fashioned Shakespearean type of play, with beginnings, middles and endings, a whole new host of bizarre opportunists, the dollop terrorists of the box office, have arrived and now lurk under the oddest of names: devisers, facilitators, co-convenors, adaptors, extemporaneous arrangers, conceptualists, collaborators, literary interns, creative associates, installators, curators, all in place but incapable of even writing a decent rejection slip, let alone a real live play - much too much like hard work. So beware England. Save yourselves from the Welsh plague 'histrionorum mortalis.' It causes disease and can prove fatal. And there is no known antidote!

**FAR FROM THE END!**

# Titles from Creative Print Publishing Ltd

## Fiction

The Shadow Line & The Secret Sharer     Joseph Conrad
ISBN 978-0-9568535-0-9

Kristina's Destiny     Diana Daneri
ISBN 978-0-9568535-1-6

Andrew's Destiny     Diana Daneri
ISBN 978-0-9568535-2-3

To Hold A Storm     Chris Green
ISBN 978-0-9568535-3-0

Ten Best Short Stories of 2011     Various
ISBN 978-0-9568535-5-4

The Lincoln Letter     Gretchen Elhassani
ISBN 978-0-9568535-4-7

Dying to Live     Katie L. Thompson
ISBN 978-0-9568535-7-8

Keeping Karma     Louise Reid
ISBN 978-0-9568535-6-1

Escape to the Country     Patsy Collins
ISBN 978-0-9568535-8-5

Lindsey's Destiny     Diana Daneri
ISBN 978-0-9568535-9-2

ANGELS UNAWARES     Dedwydd Jones
ISBN 978-1-909049-02-4

RELICK     Steven Gepp
ISBN 978-1-909049-03-1
It Hides In Darkness     Ross C. Hamilton
ISBN 978-1-909049-04-8

Transmission of Evil                        Mandy Sheering
ISBN 978-1-909049-06-2

Ransom                                      Don Nixon
ISBN 978-1-909049-07-9

Milwaukee Deep                              G. Michael
ISBN 978-1-909049-05-5

PANDORA                                     Marcus Woolcott
ISBN 978-1-909049-09-3

Shadowscape The Stevie Vegas Chronicles     M. R. Weston
ISBN 978-1-909049-10-9

Alaric, Child Of The Goths                  Daniel F. Bowman
ISBN 978-1-909049-08-6

For Catherine                               Elizabeth Morgan
ISBN 978-1-909049-01-7

**Nonfiction**
Amazonia – My Journey Into The Unknown   -   Adam Wikierski
ISBN 978-1-909049-00-0

## Contacting Creative Print Publishing Ltd

**Creative Print Publishing Limited**
17 George Street
Milnsbridge
Huddersfield
HD3 4JD
United Kingdom

w: http://www.creativeprintpublishing.com
e: info@creativeprintpublishing.com
t: +44 (0)845 868 8430